Complex Heaven

By

Richard Valanga

Published by New Generation Publishing in 2013

Copyright © Richard Valanga 2013

First Edition

The author asserts the moral right under the Copyright, Designs and Patents Act 1988 to be identified as the author of this work.

All Rights reserved. No part of this publication may be reproduced, stored in a retrieval system or transmitted, in any form or by any means without the prior consent of the author, nor be otherwise circulated in any form of binding or cover other than that which it is published and without a similar condition being imposed on the subsequent purchaser.

www.newgeneration-publishing.com

 New Generation **Publishing**

This book is dedicated to my mother Elizabeth, my father Charles and my uncle Bob.

COMPLEX HEAVEN - CONTENTS

Chapter 1   PART ONE

Chapter 2   THE BLUE VEINS

Chapter 3   HOME
                Always Returning
                Devils Wood

Chapter 4   ACCEPTANCE
                Dreams
                Post

Chapter 5   RYHOPE CHURCH
                Cherry Knowles
                Pennywell

Chapter 6   PORTAL

Chapter 7   PART TWO - THE BLACK WIRE
                Ryhope Cemetery

Chapter 8   WASHINGTON
                The Oxclose Inn

Chapter 9   THE COMRADES

Chapter 10 BRIDGE END
                Devils Wood - Midnight
                The Ghost of Devils Wood

Chapter 11 REVEREND ROBINSON
                Closure

Chapter 12 WASHINGTON LIBRARY

"WATCH THE ROADS..."

We did not buy a rose from an old Gypsy woman and this was her curse on my family... RICHMOND, LONDON 1989

PART ONE

Chapter One

The reason I came back was because I could. No, that is not exactly true... I came back because I was allowed to. I was eventually given access to a Blue Portal and that is something very special indeed; a great privilege one might say for those granted the opportunity. I was given the opportunity because I was being tormented by something I did not understand. Prayers had been entering my abode like sonic e-mails and they disturbed me. They invaded my dreams and echoed in my mind constantly throughout the day. Mumbled words by a voice I vaguely recognized began to haunt me...

Please God... Please forgive me... Help me God...Give me the strength to go on. I have fallen... and I am sick of this life... so sick that I cannot continue... Help me!

I could not ignore them... the Blue Veins of the Clear Conscious would not let me and neither would my sanity.

I had to try and get back but I was not really sure if it was possible or indeed allowed. Did I need permission? Or did Ghosts walk the Earth whenever they wanted. To freely come and go whenever they pleased? Sure, I had been intrigued by the Hereafter like a zillion others but I never actually saw any 'spirit' walking while I was alive. Strange things had happened to me though throughout my years, which I used to call Life's Little Mysteries but they never interfered with my sanity, they were just a curiosity that's all.

One such curiosity though was simply extraordinary, a paranormal experience that defied explanation to me at the time. It happened the night my mother died...

It was a sad, depressing time. I had been down on my

luck for about a year and a half and to be unemployed for that length of time is no joke, especially for a newly qualified teacher of Art with a BA Honours Degree. This is England though and that means that if you are over forty you are practically finished, especially if you are trying to make a career for yourself in a new field.

I had decided to try teaching after working in the wonderful world of Advertising for seventeen years; which when I think back I must have hated just about every second of it. Although again that is not exactly true, I quite enjoyed doing what I was employed to do and that was Graphic Design and Art Direction. What I despised was the studio politics; the back stabbers and ambitious crawlers who were prepared to do anything to further their careers. I did eventually reach the top echelon of Creative Directive at various Agencies and Design Studios but it was still the same old bull… it was not enough for a life-long frustrated Fine Artist.

THE SECRET OF LIFE is doing what you want to do, working in a job where you want to get out of bed in the morning. Of course this was my own fault; I had made the wrong choice years ago by choosing to do a Degree in Graphics rather than Fine Art. This decision though was not taken lightly; I simply thought that I could help my divorced mother financially by entering the Commercial Art industry… of course the reality was far from what I expected.

There always seemed to be a economical recession of some sort in Britain when I was young and the North East and Sunderland in particular were always one of the hardest hit. After leaving Art College, I persevered as long as I could in low paid dead end jobs and after a few years of drudgery and depression I found myself in Johannesburg, South Africa with a newly wed wife. The scene was set for success then… and it did lead to possibly the happiest four years of my working life and although it was damned hard work it did eventually pay off in the form of rapid career progress. Perhaps I had become one of those ambitious crawlers and was blind to it.

Eventually though after the novelty of the sun had dried up and was no longer a motivator, we became homesick and returned to England. I very soon found work as an Art Director in London and my life changed yet again as I took on the challenge and stress of working in a major capital city.

New friendships were formed and new experiences were gained... and one such experience that I can only describe as paranormal, was to puzzle me for the rest of my life. At the time I had no idea of how important it was going to be in relation to later events.

I had rented a house in Mortlake, near to Barnes in West London. Mortlake was reputed to be one of the most magical places in England due to the fact that many court magicians and wizards had resided there throughout the ages. Perhaps the unusual history of the place had something to do with the start of it? What I can definitely say is that Mortlake was where I first discovered my strange 'Slider' ability.

Due to the heavy traffic of London I decided that it would be easier to travel to work by bus; the old number 9 if I remember correctly. I say old because the bus was a typical seventies red London bus; the sort you could jump off and on when it was moving. You even had the bonus of bus conductors, which is sadly a symbol of bygone days now.

I used to get paid over-time in those days, which resulted in seven-day working weeks and long working hours. It was after yet another hard days work that I jumped off at my bus stop in Mortlake, which was next to an old small church, the name of which eludes me at the moment.

It was late and there was a typical London fog that night that was not heavy, just misty enough to make a lonely walk through an old graveyard just that little bit uncomfortable, even with a few pints of Guinness inside. The graveyard was a shortcut to the house where I lived and it only had one small streetlamp. I must have used this walkway many times but this night I suddenly stopped dead in my tracks directly under the small lamp...

I had froze for a moment and was not sure as to why I had stopped walking, then I looked up to the lamp and noticed that there was no light. As soon as I had stepped under the lamp it had gone out! I was alone in the darkness of a creepy old graveyard but that was not the reason I was unnerved. It was the sudden realization that this had happened many times before! I felt a cold shudder course through me but it was not the damp London fog... it was the cold awareness of something strange and mystifying...

I continued on my walk out of the churchyard towards my house, which was only two streets away and as I walked directly under the streetlights I noticed that many had gone out! As I looked behind me there was only darkness. Again it hit me; this was no coincidence, it had happened many times before and now I was aware of it!

Over the next year or so this strange phenomenon kept occurring with alarming regularity, so much so that I began to log where and when it happened. What I also began to realize was that it seemed to be more prevalent after a particularly stressful day at work.

The lights going out began to intrigue me to the point where I became slightly obsessed by it... I decided that I would take my 'research' to a university.

Initially most people did not believe me, which was understandable as I was an art director and was paid to have an active imagination. But some of them did witness it happening; they saw the light go out directly above my head and they still found it hard to believe. They knew that it was not normal but they had seen it! It was no trick... it was real and bizarre and not contrived.

Then one day I was watching a television programme about a Priest who travelled around England investigating various paranormal events... and to my great surprise and also relief, it included a report on people who were experiencing the same weird phenomenon as me. They were known as SLIDERS for some reason and of course this name puzzled me but what was really important about the report was the fact that I now knew that I was not alone!

After some time I decided that I would try and contact the Priest with the view to maybe discussing what I experienced with other Sliders but then fate intervened and the work climate of a new recession forced me back home to the North East, where the worry of what to do next became a priority.

My Slider experiences continued though...

Doesn't time fly when you're having fun... after the seemingly endless struggle of financially depressive years, Lady Luck decided to spurn me big time. In my mid-forties I found myself divorced and jobless. I had managed to qualify as a teacher of Art though during this period but could not work initially, due to the dark cloud of heavy debt that hovered constantly above my beaten head.

So I found myself in the worst place possible; a

small despondent flat in a place called Oxclose that I thought at the time probably signaled my end. The first morning in that flat, I woke up on a bare camp bed like Dracula rising from the dead…

Do you understand blues music?
I understand blues music…
I couldn't listen to anything…
Not even my favourite Family…
Or the Velvets…
Not even Waits or Eno…
Nothing I suppose that held memories of happier times.
I woke up in that flat and I had nothing!
I was nothing.
I was a failure full stop
I went to the Washington library to see if I still wanted to read…
I could not…
But I found myself looking through the blues music section…
John Lee Hooker, Muddy Waters and Howlin' Wolf…
I took them home and I listened to them…
In some ways those blues artists saved me.

I understand blues music…
Do you?

So I could have easily given in but I was a fighter; I guess I still am to this day and fighting is not just about fists and feet, oh no… the real battles go on inside the mind! My father was a fighter, he was an Army boxing champion who had gained military medals in Burma during World War II. He was a man that had been shot in the foot and then blown up by a Japanese grenade while fighting ahead of the rest of his troops. He did somehow manage to crawl back to his Division and survive though... so perhaps some of that steely grit had been handed down to me. My choice was simple then... quit or fight; I chose the latter.

As soon as I was settled in my 'fabulous' flat I was given the family dog to look after. It was heartbreaking not being able to live with my two sons JJ and Robert so Arnie the cross border collie was a constant source of companionship for me. He kept my spirits high and I went running with him regularly, which meant that I kept up my fitness for playing football. I think that I may have hinted that I was something of a skilled artist and I have to say that I was also something of an all-round sportsman too. Both these attributes helped me to survive this desolate period.

But in April 2000 Lady Luck dealt me her deadliest hand and the worst thing in my life happened... my mother died. She had suffered a heart attack at my sister's house and barely a week later she was gone from this world. I had visited my mother with both my brother and sister every day while she was in hospital and the signs were that she was recovering steadily. Indeed on the final evening, my sister Dot and I expected that our mother would be home in a few days, as she seemed so well and in good spirits. Mother had been laughing and joking with us but it was not a good spirit that was on that ward that night. We left the hospital under heavy April showers with high hopes. Hopes that were soon to be horribly dashed. I was sure that something sinister had happened, as that night I was tormented by a terrible dream...

It was not a dream though, it was a nightmare... based on something I had observed briefly during the hospital visit. Sometimes, fleeting things you see stick in your mind for no reason whatsoever but can come back to haunt you when you least expect them to. Something I saw that night triggered this nightmare...

The hospital ward was quiet and peaceful, it was nearly midnight and my mother and her fellow patients were asleep. The light in the room was dim and slightly foreboding in the moonlight... in my sleep I began to squirm and sweat, something was not right...

A face appeared in my mind... a small, thin face with shifty eyes and a pointed nose. The man's hair was blonde, slightly greasy and unkempt. It was the hospital porter I had briefly seen walk past whilst talking to my mother and he was standing at the door to the wardroom. He appeared as a dark shadow with ominous intent... the scene began to play over and over frantically in my head. The porter would walk past the open door then stop and sneer at my mother. Sometimes he moved at a faster pace, which seemed like a movie effect used in vampire horror films. This seemed to mimic my quickening heartbeat as my anxiety increased in my troubled sleep. His unsettling face became bigger and his smile sicklier... there was something about this porter that suggested that he was not human. His eyes were snake-like as he glared threateningly from the door.

The light was now a dull green and menacing, Victorian style smog suddenly filled the air as if announcing that something evil was about to happen. In the doorway the porters face contorted grotesquely so that it became demonic in appearance. There was no smile anymore, only malice. He entered the wardroom and I knew what his objective was... my mother! I tried to call out in my sleep, to warn her but I could not make a sound. I tried again and again but my screams were silent... He crept slowly towards my mother, his bony hands reaching out with cruel intent. It was like a scene from Nosferatu and it was too much for me to bear...

I woke up immediately, my sweat cold and uncomfortable. My heart was racing and thumping like it was about to break and of course it was... the phone rang and I was scared to answer it.

It was my sister Dot and she could hardly speak as she stuttered down the line... and even though she was only five miles away I could tell that there were tears in her eyes. She was coming to pick me up as our mother had passed away. I put the phone down and my first instinct was to reach for the Whisky bottle but I had to be strong. I knew that if I started drinking I would not stop. I went into a dream-like state as I waited for my sister in the dark of the night.

Nobody spoke in the car as my brother-in-law Pete drove us all to the hospital. My brother John kept a brave face but Dot could not control her grief. We entered the hospital in silence and went to the room where our mother, Elizabeth lay. It was hard to accept that she was dead, it seemed as if she was only sleeping... the hardship of life was gone from her face and she looked younger. She was at peace and we stood there like statues... figures of stone that were weeping. Our hearts were frozen and broken and changed forever.

My sister returned home and I went to my brother's house where we drank Brandy but only for about half an hour as talking seemed painful and the next morning there were many things to sort out. I think it was about 5am when I walked the short distance home.

My flat had a hallway that lead to a sliding door to the sitting room. Arnie as ever was there to greet me but before I stepped into the main room I stopped suddenly... something was holding me back.

An overpowering smell of smoke filled the air; it

was as if the room was thick of it and yet no grey smoke could be seen. I then realized that it was not the fumes from any fire or the lingering cigarette ash of recently departed burglars. No, it was the distinctive smell of pipe tobacco, so rich and strong that it could not be natural. I turned the light on and surely my sight of the room should have been obscured but it was not... the room was clear.

Tears formed in my eyes, I did not sob but my eyes were full of water that eventually fell slowly down the side of my cheeks. I kept still in the doorway and I was sure that Arnie was now worried. He was one of the most intelligent dogs I had ever known and he simply sat in the room and waited patiently for his master to enter.

I then realized that the tears that were falling were partially tears of joy and that I was laughing quietly, almost hysterically. I think I spluttered... "She is alright, she is okay." As I stood there I had realized that the tobacco odour was a sign. My mother's father had been here... that had to be the explanation as my grandfather had been the only person I knew that had smoked a pipe; I had been transported back to his house in Bevan Avenue, Ryhope by the nostalgic aroma. Somehow he had managed to get a message to me.... he was telling me not to worry; that my mother was with him and the rest of her family!

One thing is certain in this world and that is the fact that things will change... and they did. After clearing the cloud of debt, I managed to get regular work as a supply teacher. My two sons, Robert and JJ came to live with me and I finally managed to move out of that damned flat. After threatening the Company that owned the flat with a law suite for disrepair regarding the obscene dampness, they re-housed us almost immediately.

So the world became a better place for us all, including Arnie who now had a large back garden to play and relax in. JJ and Robert followed their dreams, which were music, and I followed mine, which was art and writing. I produced my most important charcoal drawings and oil paintings during this period and I even managed to write a Novel. They say that everyone has a book inside of them... it turned out that I had four; five if you include this one. I also kept playing football and even at my time of life I regularly received shouts of 'awesome' from younger players, at least I think that's what they said. Things were definitely looking up then...

After four years though, tragedy struck again. It was the start of a cold November when Arnie fell ill and as it was with my mother, within one week he had passed away. The first sign of his illness was his loss of appetite. His morning walks were suddenly traumatic for him and all he wanted to do was stay in the back garden and watch the sunset... he knew that his time had come but I did not.

I drove him to the vets in Chester-le-Street and it was there that I received the fateful news that his liver and kidneys had failed; there was nothing the vet could do. I held Arnie lovingly as they administered the poisonous serum that would take him from me. I covered his eyes with my trembling hands as he slowly slipped away without pain. My eyes were full of tears but I was not ashamed, how could I be, Arnie had been part of my family for fourteen years... and during the hard times I sometimes felt that he was the only friend I had in the world. My heart was broken and I knew that I could never go through this again.

Arnie was respectfully wrapped in thick blankets and the vet helped me put him in the back of my Fiat car. She asked if I was okay to drive, as she knew how upset I was. Of course I could drive... I had to.

I drove away slowly from that fateful place. My eyes were still watery as I drove too cautiously towards the main roundabout. Then a small speeding car came up directly behind me, the horn blaring with menace. At the point of the roundabout I started to turn left and the speeding car overtook to go straight ahead towards Shiney Row. It was full of young scumbags who were shouting at me through the windows while putting their fingers up. Perhaps I had been driving too slowly or perhaps they had seen how upset I was... whatever the reason, my intense grief turned instantly to immense anger. I could not recall such an instant change of emotion! Lucky for them though and perhaps me, I was now driving down a one way dual-carriageway to Washington, which gave me precious time to calm down.

I know now that it was just another brush with the Dark Conscious, something that happens everyday while you are alive. The Dark Conscious had taunted me...

When I arrived back home I had to break the sad news to my two sons. Robert helped me bury Arnie in the back garden, in his favourite place but JJ was just too upset and went straight to his room. Before we placed Arnie in his final resting place, we looked at his peaceful face for the last time and like my mother he looked like he was only sleeping, perhaps dreaming. Perhaps death is only just a dream... I was soon to find out.

Two years later on my birthday, I died.

Chapter Two

THE BLUE VEINS

It was a sunny September day at the end of an Indian summer. Friday, and no one had called on me to work. This meant a light lunch of sausage, bacon, egg and tomatoes before an energetic game of football. My good friend Steve Nanson had rang to update me about our joint venture in Seaburn. We were in the process of opening a diner on the seafront. This was going to be a dream come true as I would probably have to retire from teaching, which meant that I could have more time to write and paint. The diner had been my vision but Steve had the money to finance it. He had decided to retire from Advertising and had relocated with his wife Jacqui, back to his beloved Sunderland from Edinburgh. Steve had rung to discuss the photographic portraits we were going to use for atmospheric effect. I was really excited by what we were doing and was sure that the diner was going to be a big success. So it was football first then a few pints with Steve later.

At 3.10, I set off in my black Fiat Punto towards the school where we regularly played. Ten minutes later I pulled off the A1231 Sunderland Highway at the Wessington Pub and proceeded up Ferryboat Lane on the edge of Castletown. At the end of this road was a junction that preceded a short, sharp bend to the left where the speed limit increased dramatically.

My Ultimate Nick Cave CD was playing Clean Hands Dirty Hands from the movie, The Proposition. I needed to turn right but my sight of the road was partially blocked by a large, black Station Wagon that was side parked on the pavement. I looked left and it was clear... I looked right and it was clear. I was about to place my foot down on the pedal, when the Station Wagon started to move... I stayed put until the Wagon indicated that it was turning left to go down Ferryboat Lane. The road was clear when I pulled out...

Then light...
Not white light... it was blue.
As blue as a deep ocean...
I was swimming and the water was warm...
Fish and dolphins swam with me...
I was heading to...?
Then shadows in the distance...
Wriggling with menace...
I thought they were sharks...

Slowly the water turned darker...
Green mist above restless waves...
Like a Victorian smog...

Someone was waving a large white flag...
With a cross that was red.
I swam ashore...
To a lonely beach...
There was no one...
No flag...
Just a red cross in the sand...
I touched it...
It was not paint it was blood!
Fresh and thick...
I stood back... my hands dripping...

I was standing...
Looking out to sea...
But there was no water...
There was nothing...

There was even no pain and...
I felt like I was floating...
But my feet touched cold ground.
There was no memory of my car or where I was going.
Only a blue light above me now...
and a dark green circling smog below.
My mind was confused as I tried to move.
My feet stuck in a swirling jelly.
My legs were frozen...
I looked at them and there was wire attached to them.
Black tentacles were rising from the green mist
Moving like menacing snakes...
Wrapping around my legs.

I was being pulled down... into the grimy smog...
I did not know who I was; something had connected with my bewildered brain.
I felt evil...
Dark thoughts entered my mind.
I began to laugh. It felt like laughter, perhaps it was fear.
I did not like where this nightmare was taking me...

I felt like I was changing... Dr Jeykll to Mr. Hyde.

A black and white movie scene...

Mr. Hyde was in a bar, a smoky bar he recognized. It was not a pub though, it was a working-mans club. Mr. Hyde looked around... it was full of people drinking, laughing, enjoying themselves. Why was he here? He hated happy people! They were Trolls that should be punished...
Mr. Hyde was thirsty... he walked up to the bar like he owned it.
He wanted Guinness, Gin... Drugs and he wanted them

at once!
Mr. Hyde pushed to the front, not caring who was in his way.
Some men moved but others stood their ground.
To Mr. Hyde they were not men; they were Trolls and Ogres... long hair, short hair, and ugly tattoos. Mr. Hyde hated meaningless, ugly tattoos.
The Trolls began to crowd him...
Move, move... get away from me, you are not worthy!
The Trolls closed in...

Mr. Hyde grabbed a brown ale bottle and smashed it against the bar top.
Keep away Scum of the Earth...
Filthy Ogres...
But they did not heed his words...
Mr. Hyde lashed out at them with the broken bottle. He slashed at their throats and their eyes and it felt good!
Music played in the back of his mind...
Clean Hands and Dirty Hands...
They fell back in horror screaming... this man was mad!
This man was evil...
The Trolls were scared... and so was Mr. Hyde...
He was not himself... not who he was really was...

Then the Blue Veins appeared...
That is what they seemed like... living, translucent veins that attached themselves to my body.
They had come from above and hooked onto me...
I think that they may have been there all the time... I began to relax.
I was floating...

Mr. Hyde was changing back...

Then there was pain... immense and searing...
I was being stretched... pulled from above and below.
In my mind I was Mr. Fantastic...
being stretched to the limit.
The pain came from the Black Wire, it would not let go...

Then my mind snapped... like a blue firework display
Whiz... Bang... Crackle...

Silence...
Peace...
I was lying down and the Dark Light had gone.
My body was normal...

Mr. Fantastic was himself and he wanted to fly.
I knew I could fly.
I had dreamt it so many times before...
recurring... and I welcomed it.
I reached my arms up to the warm wind and asked it to carry me...
I left the ground...
swimming strokes upward... with little effort
the wind was the water...
Floating above the trees, I was not scared of heights anymore
as I looked down to the calm world below.
I swam and flew over fields of different colours, a moving miniature maze...
Then over the city and towards the sea...
but that was not my destination...
I turned back... I was looking for something
like a proud eagle, scanning for prey.
I was looking for...
myself.
I glided back inland...

floated over Castletown
then slowly down...
and rested...

Chapter Three

HOME

I sat up by the side of a road I vaguely recognized, I was holding on tightly to the silver cross and Saint Christopher that had been around my neck since I was nineteen. This comforted me but I did not know why. There was no memory of Mr. Hyde or Mr. Fantastic, no red and white flag.

I knew it was warm yet I did not feel warm. It was a lovely, sunny day yet the source of the sun was obscure. I stood up and tried to remember where I was and where I was going. I was dressed in sports kit; a red and white striped football shirt and black tracksuit bottoms, my trainers were Puma.

The road I was sitting beside was quiet and strangely deserted so I stood up and crossed it. My movement was slow and cautious, almost as if I had never walked before and that was a strange sensation indeed. There were houses in the distance that were gently shrouded in a light blue haze. These dwellings were of all shapes and sizes; there was no conformity to their build. When I reached the pavement I looked back; it felt like it had taken an eternity to walk a few paces. I thought that I must have been dreaming. I stood awhile and looked around... no movement of any sort. It must have been Sunday I remember thinking... then I heard the ruffle of feathers above me. A bird was flying past, high above me but it was not a species I recognized. It was a tropical bird I was sure and not one that was found in this region. In slow motion it flew gracefully towards the blue haze but there was no wind, no breeze and this made its flight seem unnatural.

Time seemed to melt as I as stood there staring at

the faraway buildings. I was aware that I was definitely in some kind of a dream-like state as my mind soaked up the beautiful scenery. Everything seemed to sparkle in the distance... everything seemed new and exciting. I seemed to remember a location like this but that was another place, another time.

Then I heard a car quietly approaching behind me. A white BMW pulled up slowly beside me. It was open topped and inside sat a young man who smiled at me then enquired...

"Can I help...?"

"I... I'm not sure." I was confused but I was calm and not afraid.

"Perhaps you have just wandered too far. It can happen easily here. I can take you home if you want."

"Home?" A building appeared in my mind but not the address... "Yes, I should go home..."

"Come on then friend, get in. My wish is your command."

I opened the car door and got in. The stranger gave me a broad smile and then we were off.

"Where to then?" my new friend asked.

I had to concentrate... think hard...

"My home... my home is in... Washington. Do you know where that is?"

"Yes, I have been there... a long time ago. The road we need used to be the 1231."

We turned left at the junction I had been standing on and preceded down a long road towards the buildings in the blue haze. The car was smooth and silent. We glided past the distant houses to the left of us... I felt that there was someone living there who knew me but I could not remember who it was. But the decision had been made; I was on my way home... and soon we were at a large roundabout.

"We turn right here... it should not take us long"

said my Good Samaritan.

I looked at him while he drove us along a wide, open highway that was reminiscent of the kind you find in America. He was as young as me with short, light brown hair that was combed back in a definite thirties style. His profile reminded me of a young Robert Mitchum; the fact that I knew who Mitchum was did not quite register with me at the time. My driver had a kind face, the face of someone who was content with life and with a car like this why shouldn't he be I thought. I kept staring at him because I was sure that I recognized him from somewhere. There were tattoos on his arms that were vaguely familiar... two bluebirds above a snake and dagger. These tattoos seemed to suggest a military connection of some sort and yet he did not seem old enough. He did not seem to mind my inquisitive glare; he just smiled and concentrated on the road ahead.

His blue eyes were very striking. There seemed to be an inner light behind them, a brightness that was bursting to get out...

"Do you mind if I put the radio on?" he enquired.

"Of course not" I said, "I love music."

He pressed a button and Radio Three the Classical Station came on. I recognized the music but could not recall what the title was. A vision of a man (I now remember as Robert De Niro) entered my mind. He was standing in the shadows, looking down to a lonely house where people he knew were leaving. He was an American soldier returning from the Viet Nam war and it was early morning and he was alone. It was the theme from The Deer Hunter but I did not know it at the time.

"I thought you would be more of a Radio One sort, you look too young for Classical music" I joked. He turned to look at me and his eyes seemed brighter than before.

"Oh, I am not as young as you might think..." he quietly stated, then turned back and continued to drive. The music continued in the background and gently eased my troubled mind... but something began to happen as we headed along the highway, the perfect weather began to change. Slowly at first they came, storm clouds in the distance that were dark and menacing. I could hear the sound of rumbling thunder and see the angry lightning as it struck the landscape with rage...

"That's some storm coming" I exclaimed and as I turned to see my drivers reaction I was stunned by who was now sitting there... it was not the young man with the kind face, he was somebody different, somebody that seemed instantly loathsome to me. My first impression of this man was that he was some grotesque Mister Hyde and the fact that he was now driving the car instead of my kind new friend, completely threw me... but I somehow had to keep my head, as I was well aware that I was hallucinating for some reason...

"Lets change the station shall we... liked the movie, especially the Russian roulette scenes but not the soppy music. Lets see if we can find The Doors or Nick Cave..." he slobbered as he frantically fidgeted with the radio dial. The lightning storm was now directly overhead but I noticed that there was no rain just a venomous wind that began to batter the car dangerously...

"Where... are we going?" I pleaded and he turned to face me with a look of pure contempt...

"Why I'm taking you home stupid, where do you think we're going. I got better things to do than to drive you around all day..." He turned his gaze back to the road and I was glad as his eyes held an evil hatred within them, the like of which I had never seen before.

But there was still something familiar about this monstrosity of a man, something that was beyond the reach of my muddled mind.

We pulled off the motorway and turned left into a housing estate...

"This is it, here will do..." I shouted in relief... but Mister Hyde drove on.

I looked back out of the window, I was sure we had passed my street...

"You don't live there you ungrateful dog, this is where you belong!"

We suddenly pulled sharp left and then stopped abruptly...

"Get out, you've kept me from my pleasures too long. There's your stinking flat there. Go before I'm tempted to..." he did not have to say anymore, I jumped out of that car as quick as I could... but where was I? Mister Hyde drove off at a manic pace, the tyres of the car screeching loudly as he went. I was so relieved but now also so alone. There was nobody about, only the whipping wind and the electric storm above. Then I knew where I was, I had lived here before but that was now so long ago surely. I was standing in front of a rundown neglected block of flats and the corner apartment was mine. Suddenly I was aware of the birds flying around the building, they seemed scared of the dark raging elements that were bombarding them. Wood pigeons were scurrying in flight to and fro while above them large seagulls swooped in for the kill. Magpies that sounded like rattlesnakes, scuttled frantically for cover then I heard a low growling sound behind me, I turned swiftly to face a large rabid dog that had the look of a wolf about it. The creature was creeping dangerously towards me with hungry eyes that suggested that Mister Hyde had just delivered its next meal. I ran to the door of the flat as quick as I could with the slavering beast snapping at my heels.

Luckily for me the door was not locked and once inside I slammed it shut immediately. I leant back against the door to regain my breath... what was this Hell I had arrived at! I tried to compose myself; whatever was going on I knew that I was going to have to be strong. I was standing in the hallway staring at the walls that were almost black with unhealthy dampness aware that unwelcome recollections were beginning to return. I went to the sliding door that led into the sitting room and pushed it to one side. I did not enter immediately though... I simply stood and tried hard to remember. What was waiting for me inside I did not know; for the moment there was too many memories that would not surface.

I entered the room and the smell was almost unbearable. This was not right; it was never as bad as this. What was I doing here? I was beginning to panic... there was nobody in the flat but I felt that there should have been. I looked around the room and it was almost bare save for an old TV and an orange settee. There were no personal artifacts, no photographs, nothing to trigger anything inside of me. I went to the main bedroom and it was the same... empty apart from an old bed. I then went to the bathroom and then the kitchen, everything was cold and damp; even my breath seemed visible as I breathed out the horrid stench.

I was beginning to crumble inside, I knew that I could not be strong for much longer. Perhaps I was being punished for some reason or perhaps it was all just a bad dream and I would wake up soon, how I hoped that this was true. As I stood in the kitchen like a sad lonely old soul, I became aware of the sound of whispering voices but they were not inside the apartment. I opened the kitchen window blinds and then stepped back... people of all ages with pallid faces were standing outside as rigid as zombies and looking into the flat like there was something inside they wanted. The storm cackled like an old witch above them. They looked dead and lost... my bad dream was getting worse! There was so many of them it was frightening, they stretched back across the road to the houses in the distance. Everywhere I looked, dark black eyes looked back. Suddenly I felt I was one of them, it was as if they were beckoning me to join them. I staggered back into the living room and collapsed onto the sofa. I curled up into a ball like a child that was trying to hide and shut my eyes as tight as I could...

"No more... no more" I stuttered, "please let me wake up God!"

I was pleading for help, pleading for my sanity.

How long I lay like that I do not know but what broke me from my fear was a smell I remembered from my youth... the aroma of my grandfathers pipe! It comforted me and gave me hope. This was not where I lived; I lived somewhere else...

I opened my eyes and I was back in the white BMW, my friendly driver was smoking a cigarette...

"Are you okay son? You went a little silent there for a moment," he said with concern.

"I'm... yes, I'm okay now. I just want to get home."

We reached the end of the motorway and pulled off at a small slip road.

"Where to now then? If we had carried on we would have ended up in Newcastle"

I was slightly disorientated and asked the blue-eyed man to slow down...

"Yes we are close, left here I think... I know it is not far from here."

We went a few more yards then I said "Right... I recognize this road."

We pulled into Bridge End but it seemed different. I knew it was the right place though, I could sense it.

At the end of the road we stopped, it was a cul-de-sac and we were at the bottom of a long driveway.

"This is it, I am sure."

We both looked to the house at the end of Bridge End and smiled.

"It seems much bigger than I expected..." I exclaimed.

"Are you sure this is it? I have all the time in the world you know. Perhaps I used to be a taxi driver."

My driver laughed at this statement as I reached inside my tracksuit pockets...

"I'm afraid I don't seem to have any money on me. If you would wait..."

This made the young man laugh even louder...

"Don't worry son, money is the least of our worries now."

I stepped out of the car, and then he turned it around...

"I can't thank you enough. Do you want to come in for a refreshing drink; I am sure there will be something nice and cool inside."

"No thanks son, I have things to do, horses to attend..."

"Perhaps you will drop by some other day then?"

"Yes, perhaps I will. I am sure we will meet again. When you have settled in maybe?"

'Settled in' seemed an unusual thing to imply considering I was home but there was no time to ponder this. As my new friend began to pull away he asked me...

"By the way son, what is your name?"

"I... I'm afraid I don't recall..."

"Don't worry, I'm sure it will come back to you, it usually does…"

Then he was off, back on his way to…? I called out to him that I did not know his name but he was gone. I watched him drive to the end of the road then something nagged at me… why did he keep calling me son?

I realized that I was standing still and daydreaming, staring into space like some mindless zombie trying to remember something. Then I became conscious of the neighbours, what would they think? I turned towards the house. It was a modest detached house with a large garage to the right. I walked up the drive past tall rose bushes that displayed every colour, to the front door… it was number 55. I had no keys on me but luckily the door was not locked. I opened it and stepped inside…

"Hello… is anybody home?" I tentatively enquired. I was not sure whom I was expecting to answer but there was only silence. I think I expected a dog to bark but it did not. The only sound I heard was that of the birds singing at the back of the house.

I walked down the hallway past the kitchen to a white door and opened it. It was the sitting room but it was empty. A large room greeted me then that was bright and bare and full of light… I was definitely home but where was everything?

I went to the door that led to the garden. The upper half of the door had small square windows that I could look through. The garden was large and simply divided into two sides by a pathway that led to a wooden door. This door was set in a tall fence that was overgrown with green vines. In fact the whole garden was overgrown and neglected. I opened the door and stepped outside.

Birds were singing but I could not see them. I imagined them to be Bluebirds as the image of my

Good Samaritans tattoo suddenly filled my memory. I looked up towards a bright blue sky that was cloudless... again there was no source of sunlight. I was standing on a concrete path and there was no shadow. I listened for the voices of neighbours but none was heard... it was so peaceful, so quiet.

I went back inside the house and went to the kitchen, I was not hungry just curious. Like the sitting room it was bare... I opened the cupboards and they were all empty, I opened the fridge and it was bare too. It was if nobody had lived here... I felt a strange shudder pass through me. I felt that the house was waiting for something, waiting for someone to inhabit it. The tingling sensation I had imagined was the realization that the house had been waiting for me.

I went up the hallway stairs where there were three large bedrooms and a bathroom. I was not surprised to find that all the rooms were empty apart from the first bedroom that did have a single bed and mattress.

I felt that this was my room for some reason as I sat and relaxed on the soft mattress. My body did not feel tired... my mind however, needed to rest. I was not anxious, not afraid. I knew something had happened but I did not know what. I now know that I was not ready to face up to the facts... something instinctive was protecting me. I had to rest and recharge my batteries.

It was dark now and the stars were out. Not white stars but beautiful blue ones that shone their twinkling light into my room. There was no moon but the night comforted me. I lay down on my small bed... and eventually drifted off to sleep. There was music in the air, gentle music that was coming from the sitting room below me...

Always Returning

Do ghosts dream? Do they remember?

In my sleep my house came back to me. The décor, the kitchen, the sitting room... all more or less as it used to be except the two other bedrooms; they remained bare and a mystery.

I sat up. I was awake and it was as if this was new to me. My mind was muddled, almost afraid as it tried to come to grips with where I was. I could not feel my heart beating and that was worrying but daylight was pouring through the window and I needed to rise.

I stood up and I was still in the same sports clothes... I needed fresh clothes. I went to my wardrobe and it was full, I checked my set of drawers and they were full, as was my shoe rack and hat shelves. I put on a white T-shirt and faded blue jeans then left my bedroom. I opened the airing cupboard and it was full of fresh linen, the bathroom had towels and soap but when I checked the other two bedrooms... they were empty. No trace of anything or anyone... no memories swirled there, only loneliness. I felt that I was home now but there was only me.

I went down stairs to the kitchen... the fridge was now full of food but I was not hungry. That was strange because I knew that I was a firm believer in breakfast, "Your body is an engine Richard, don't forget that" my mother always said. Then I heard a dog barking... I went to the front room and the garden door where scratching sounds now accompanied the barking... I opened the door...

A large, thickset border collie jumped up at me and began to lick my face. A broad smile beamed from me as I held and stroked the dog. I knew this dog and I knew he was called Arnie. We stepped out into the garden and Arnie ran around it in wild abandonment. He fetched me a small ball, which I threw for him, his bark was loud and joyful which made me feel so good. Troubled thoughts seemed dissipate as I sat on a red and white garden chair and watched my dog play. It was obvious that he had not seen me for sometime and I sat there for hours throwing his ball for him, he did not seem to tire. Arnie had boundless energy when it came to fetch and throw but unfortunately I did not. I was sure that it was time for lunch so I went hastily to the kitchen, Arnie followed with his tail wagging happily behind him.

I made myself a corned beef and onion sandwich and a refreshing cup of tea. I then opened a tin of Chum for Arnie, which he greedily gulped down in one go. I, however struggled with my snack; it was tasteless and even the onions had no bite to them which was unusual. The food had definite substance but it was different to what I was expecting. It seemed then that I had lost my sense of taste and that was... disappointing. As I finished my sandwich I thought about my sense of smell. I opened a bottle of milk and put my nose to it... nothing. My breath should have smelt of onions but it did not... there was no breath! I felt scared, like the beginning of an anxiety attack... I lifted the palm of my hand to my mouth and blew on it but there was no cool gust to soothe me. I began to panic, what else was missing! I could hear, I could see... I nipped my hand vigorously but there was no pain! This made no sense and yet I knew it did. I pulled out a sharp knife from the cutlery drawer and... slowly cut my hand. Not only was there was no pain... there was no blood! This sent my mind reeling and I knew that my heart should have been racing but it was not. I went to the main room and sat down on the brown leather sofa that faced the fireplace. Arnie sat down beside my feet, he was quiet and looked sad... he knew that something had shocked me.

I looked to the fireplace and imagined a fire burning. It was not winter and no fire ignited; in my mind though I was watching soothing flames flicker between decorative stones and coals. Questions were now burning inside of me and just sitting about would not solve them. I stood up and decided to go for a walk with Arnie. I clipped a blue leader to his red studded collar and we left the house. I still had no door keys but there was no need to lock up and I knew it.

Devils Wood

It was a short walk to the park and I noticed that the surroundings were serene and quiet. Many people were sitting on the soft green grass and were having picnics and playing with their children and pets; it was a typical summers day and an idyllic scene which helped calm my troubled spirit.

We walked past a wooded area and I let Arnie off his lead. He was not a violent dog but I remembered that he was courageous and would never run from any dogfight. I made sure that I kept my eye on him as he ran about exploring.

We were next to Devils Wood and it made me wonder why it was called that. Children of various ages were playing amongst the shaded trees; they had built a bike and skateboard track and were happy in the wood. Perhaps they had named the wooded area themselves... children always like to scare each other.

We walked on further and past people I did not recognize. The species of birds that flew around the park were varied and striking, at odds with their British surroundings. At one point I even thought I saw an Eagle, soaring majestically in the distance. Did they nest here or were they just passing?

Further ahead of me, Arnie had stopped at a pathway junction that was marked by a large engraved stone. He was wagging his tail to signal that someone he knew was approaching. A small white dog appeared and greeted Arnie... it was a lively little thing who was being followed casually by a young man.

He looked at me and smiled, it was obvious that he seemed to know me. He was smartly dressed and I sensed that he was ex Army or Navy perhaps.

"Well it is good to see Arnie again," said the man as he patted my dog on the head. I was surprised that he knew Arnie because at first I did not recognize him.

"It is good see to see you too Richard. Good to see that you and Arnie are reunited again."

He knew my name... and that was when things began to flood back. There was a wooden park seat beside the large stone and I had to sit down. The young man sat down beside me and sighed as he began to speak to me...

"Oh I see that you are still a bit confused. I'm sorry, I did not realize how long..."

"Please, do not worry. I... I now realize where I am. It seems that I have been a bit of a fool... I accept it now. I'm afraid though that my memory has not fully returned yet... I still don't recognize you."

"Of course, it is better that way. Do not force your memories to return too soon Richard... you might twist and distort them and that will haunt you."

These seemed wise words but I still did not know who was speaking them...

"Think back Richard... sunny walks on colder days. I was a little bit older but we used to have pleasant chats about football and cricket and sometimes my War experiences..."

I remembered his face but not his name...

"Aye, I can see that it will take a bit of time but you will remember. Sometimes people do not and that is sad."

Another man who had a distinctive Forces feel about him too, came along the path and joined us. Again he was pleased to see me but soon realized that I had not yet fully come to terms with where I was. Their names still eluded me but I could tell that these were two old friends that were now eternal companions.

The two men decided to continue on their walk, they knew that they would see me again and thought it was best that I was left to my own thoughts for the time being. I sat on that park bench and watched the light fade. In my mind it was raining. I did realize where I was now and it was hard to accept.

Eventually the blue stars came out and I decided to go home but there was no spring in my step as I walked back home with Arnie. Once inside the house I looked into the mirror above my seventies style phone. I no longer looked fifty-five... I was twenty one again! I went straight to the drinks cupboard and was pleased to find what I wanted, Bombay Sapphire. I poured myself a large gin and tonic and held it teasingly for a moment. It seemed like I had not been drunk for a long, long time but tonight I was going to try my damnedest.

I took a large swig of my drink and was disappointed that there was no taste... still, the sensation was the same and that was all that mattered. I took the blue bottle of gin to the main room and sat on the sofa in the blue evening light... I placed a FAMILY CD on my hi-fi and pressed SHUFFLE. BURNING BRIDGES from FEARLESS came on...

Visions they're dancing like puppets on strings
Wait for the face in the choir to sing

Cymbals and symbols you clang in my ear
While rain clouds burst out into tears

Burning your bridges on Gods Holy Fire
And all of the children you sire

Over and over my blues start to roll
Bypass my body head straight for my soul...

The gin and the music helped me...
Helped me to remember...

I staggered up the stairs drunk...
"Well... at least you can still get legless here..." I mumbled. I passed my bedroom and opened the adjacent door. The room was still empty... I went to the other bedroom and that was vacant too. It was too much for me to take; I slumped to the floor, my drink still in my hand but I had spilt it on the bare wooden boards... I began to get angry and began to shout...
"Why lord... why? There was still so much for me to do... The lads, how will they cope...? I do not deserve this, it was not my time!"
I struck the floor repeatedly, as hard as I could... there was no pain. But my heart was hurting... I knew it was.
I must have knelt there sobbing for some time, when I noticed that Arnie was licking my cheek. I put my arm around him and hugged him tightly...
"I know son, you are missing them too..." I whispered.
I stood up and went to my bed. As soon as my head hit the pillow, the room began to spin...
...and I dreamt.
Dreamt of my two sons.
Two small boys playing outside...

Kicking footballs...
Playing computer games...
Playing guitars...

In my sleep they came back to me... and in the morning...
I knew that I was dead.

Chapter Four

ACCEPTANCE

When I awoke the next morning, it felt like I had overslept and perhaps I had. I looked out of the window to another bright blue day. Arnie was sitting waiting for me.

"Hello son... come on, I'll let you into the garden."

I was pleased to note that I did not have a hangover. It must be Heaven then I thought; drink as much as you want and you will not get sick. This made me chuckle as I went to the garden with Arnie. It was all well and good making jokes about it but what was I to do now. Of course at the time I had not yet grasped that I had an eternity to do whatever I wanted but it was much too early to come to terms with such a concept.

I sat down on my garden chair and again a multitude of questions began to fill my head. I knew that it was going to be pointless trying to understand where I was or what I was but there were things that I would soon have to face up to like...

Where was my mother... my father? Where were my grandparents and my uncle Bob?

I stood up to go to the garage... then I stopped suddenly. It might be too much of a shock for them for me to suddenly just turn up on their doorstep... perhaps if I rang them first? What were their numbers? I could not remember. Then a thought hit me. Surely they would have known... I remembered the night that my mother died and my grandfathers pipe smoke in the flat. Then a cold reality hit me... perhaps they were gone. Moved away from where they had lived, surely Heaven was a place to be explored! What if I could never find them... then I truly would be alone. This thought scared me. Scared me so much that I was frightened of going to see them and finding that they were not there!

The real reason; though I did not realize it at the time, was that I was simply not yet ready to meet my dead parents... not really ready to be dead myself!

I slumped back into my chair; perhaps Lady Luck had followed me here. That just wouldn't surprise me at all! Still, I had Arnie though... my own house and my own life...

"It's life Jim but not as we know it..." suddenly entered my thoughts and I had to chuckle... this broke my mood and made me decisive. When the time was right I would try to contact them.

I did not have to wait too long...

DREAMS

For the next few weeks I was in a kind of Shangri-La. I spent time reading the books that I never got the chance to finish. I played my beloved music none stop, I wrote and I painted. It was an ideal bohemian existence... a female partner would have made my afterlife perfect I surmised. Now then, how many dead girlfriends were available...

This urge for companionship did compel me to take a walk down to Fatfield Bridge. Here there were three pubs and a working-mans club all in a row, one after the other. The ideal location then, for a short pub-crawl. I had always thought that this was quite unique considering that the pubs were situated quite a few miles from any town centre. I suppose it was something to do with the old pit village community and also the bridge being a link across the river. Four watering holes alongside the picturesque Wear, was perfect for any sunny day and that was something that seemed be guaranteed now.

The walk took us about thirty minutes through peaceful parks that again were full of people relaxing in the tranquil day. Arnie acquainted himself with many other dogs and I was sure that there were some that he remembered and knew. Thankfully he did not get into a fight with any of them, so perhaps even the dogs were at peace now.

The first building we came to was the Fatfield Working-mans Club and as we passed the open car park to the left of it I was struck by the variety of cars that were parked there. It was like a classic car convention and it was a real treat to the eye. As we walked past the wide windows of the club I noticed how full it was... what day was it? And did that even matter now! Men were sitting laughing and enjoying a pint, they were probably working out their bets for the day and playing dominoes. Many were smoking heavily and enjoying it, I suppose their days of worrying about the health risks were now obviously behind them. There was an obvious lack of women in the bar and the scene was reminiscent of the seventies I thought as a feeling of nostalgia swept over me. This bar scene was very enticing...

But I decided that Arnie might prefer somewhere quieter so we went into the next pub, which was called The Hillsdown. It was a good choice as the pub was not as crowded and I was able to get a seat on an old leather chair beside the window. Arnie settled immediately beside me as if he was tired from the walk, which again posed questions that could wait. I knew that he would watch my seat for me while I went to the bar to buy a drink and get Arnie a bowl of water.

Music was playing on a fifties style jukebox while I waited for service. I recognized the song; it was a cover version by Bryan Ferry called WALK A MILE IN MY SHOES. Very appropriate I thought, as Bryan Ferry was a famous son of Washington. I knew I had my wallet with me but no idea of how much money was in it, I had forgot to check. Surely I had enough for one pint. Two barmaids were serving and I waited patiently for my turn...

"Okay Pet, what can I get you?"

There was only one answer to that and that was a cool pint of Guinness. While the barmaid poured my drink she enquired...

"I have not seen you in here before, do you live in Fatfield or are you searching?"

This question made me feel a little self-conscious; it made me realize that I had not had a conversion with a female for some time...

"Searching? No... I live in Washington, I... it feels like I have not been in here for a long time."

"Oh I'm sorry love, I didn't realize... I should be able to tell by now. Here is your drink and your dog's water. Relax and enjoy it, there is nothing to worry about anymore."

"Yes, I suppose you are right..."

She placed my dark pint and Arnie's bowl of water in front of me and I took out my wallet...

"You do not need that... there is no need anymore. Cheers."

She then went off to serve somebody else.

I sat back down beside Arnie and looked out of the window. The old steel bridge across the river was exactly how I remembered it. The bridge shone brightly in the daylight reflecting an abstract image onto the shimmering water below. I felt compelled to paint it there and then and was a little surprised when paints and canvas did not materialize right in front of me. It was a wonderful world I now inhabited, that's for sure but it was still not quite a fairy tale as an Earthy existence still prevailed.

I was at ease in this pub although I knew that it was one I never frequented enough previously. I decided that this could be my 'local' from now on, something that had been lacking in my life in the 'old days' and a feeling of contentment came over me.

As I sat enjoying my Guinness, I looked around at the other clientele. Of course the majority of the pub crowd looked young but there were older looking people and this intrigued me... perhaps they preferred the look of maturity, to keep those hard earned facial lines that displayed a sense of character. Whatever the reason, it added to an aura of normality.

Then I looked to the children that were in the pub and thought that perhaps there was a limit as to how far you could go back in appearance and age. Surely these were children then that had sadly been taken too early in life. I pondered this for a moment as again new questions as to how the scheme of things worked here began to intrigue me. Deceased members of their family were probably looking after them I deduced. Perhaps their spirit would grow older or could it be that they were eternally stuck in the innocence of their youth. Maybe that was a better place to be.

Time drifted in the pub and so did I... as I sat thinking about my own childhood. Marvel comics and Subutteo... football honours for Sunderland Boys, they were golden times and I knew that I had been lucky. Then my quiet reflection was broken by the barmaid's voice...

"There you go; I am sure that you are ready for another pint. I brought your dog some more water and a beef and onion sandwich for you, I'm sure you remember how they tasted."

"Thanks, that's kind of you. Arnie appreciates it too.

I was just reminiscing..."

"Yes, we tend to do a lot of that... but life goes on. There is so much to enjoy now and I love this work because of the social aspect. The majority of people that come in here are content, every day is a new celebration which is great to be part of."

"Yes, I can understand that..."

"My name's Jeannette... Jeannette Alderson, and you are..."

"My name is Richard... er Richie."

"Well Mr. Richard Richie, I hope you will not be a stranger from now on. This is my pub now so I will always be here... well, for the foreseeable future anyway."

"It's a nice pub, good choice of music too."

Jeannette smiled, "a Roxy fan eh? That sort of gives your age away... I think we may have a few things in common you and I..."

She then turned slowly away and sauntered sexily back to the bar. My eyes followed her every move. Jeannette was a small, good-looking woman with a thin model figure that seemed to tease me as she walked. She had straight dark hair and brown eyes but you know what, I think I wasn't too bad looking either in my youth...

It was time to get back home though as I was sure Arnie was ready for his dinner. I went to the toilet out of habit but nothing happened, I don't think I was concentrating enough. I had to smile, as it was as if someone was next to me and the plumbing had shut down. But as I stood there, waiting and watching I noticed something unusual in front of me... a large chalkboard above the urinal. This was obviously meant to be a vehicle for light relief and it did have some very interesting pieces of graffiti wisdom. Children had obviously drawn funny faces on it but my only thought was of Jeannette and the Terminator film... I chalked up *I'LL BE BACK...*

Before I left the pub I waved to Jeannette and she smiled and waved back. Yep, I definitely would return and soon. I walked out into the glorious daylight with Arnie and I began to whistle... I think I sang Bob Dylan's THINGS HAVE CHANGED just about all the way home...

A worried man with a worried mind
No one in front of me and nothing behind
There's a woman on my lap and she's drinking champagne
That white skins got assassins eyes
I'm looking up into the sapphire tainted skies
I'm wide glassed waiting for the last train
Standing on the gallows with my head in a noose
Any minute now I'm expecting all hell to break loose

People are crazy and times are strange
I'm locked in tight, I'm out of range
I used to care but things have changed

Lot of water under the bridge, lot of other stuff too.
Don't get up gentlemen I'm only passing through
I've been walking 40 miles of bad road
If the Bible is right the world will explode
I've been trying to get as far away from myself as I can
Something's are too hot to touch
The human mind can only stand so much
You can't win with the losing hand
Feel like falling in love with the first woman I meet
Putting her in a wheelbarrow and wheeling her down the street...

Ha ha ha…

> *I hurt easy I just don't show it*
> *You can hurt someone and not even know it*
> *The next 60 seconds could be like an eternity*
> *Gonna get low down, gonna fly high*
> *All the truth in the world adds up to one big lie*
> *I'm in love with a woman that don't even appeal to me…*

Things were fine then…

I resigned myself to an idealistic lifestyle and perhaps Jeanette would play her part in that but one thing did prey on my mind though, like the eagle I had saw over Devils Wood and that was… what had happened to me? I had been fit and healthy, surely it had not been a heart attack! Try as hard as I could, I simply could not remember… I concluded that it must be some part of the healing process and that I was not ready to remember. So I left it at that. Life and death was something I was slowly beginning to enjoy. I was free to pursue my dreams and Jeannette…

And then the nightmares started.

I had gone to bed early one night as I had decided that I would go and see my parents the following day. However, as soon as I was asleep I knew that I was not in my new Heaven…

I was walking in the park but Arnie was not with me….

The constant blue sky was a cold blue...
A dark blue that was sinister and foreboding.
Lightning crackled in the distance and thunder rumbled.

A storm was approaching...
Music played softly in the background...

> *Riders on the Storm...*
> *Into this house we're born, into this house we're thrown.*
> *There's a killer on the road*
> *His brain is squirming like a toad...*

A frog jumped in front of me.
It began to rain...
A sensation that was full of memories
Water on skin, cold, cooling, refreshing...

I walked further on and the storm kept its distance...
Then lightning flashed over Devils Wood.
I stopped... I thought I saw something
Thought I heard something...

> *Take a long holiday... let your children play.*
> *If you give this man a ride, sweet memory will die...*

There were no children in Devils Wood
All was dark until the moon rose over the trees...
I watched the moon... I remembered the moon...
And there in the shadows of the black, bare trees
Stood a small girl... dressed in a white skirt of red roses...

> *Help me somebody... please help me... I'm so sorry...*

A pleading voice entered my head. So clear and heartfelt that I felt like crying.

The young girl stood still while the pleading voice

continued.
But it was not her that was calling for help.
It was a man's voice... trembling, faltering.
A voice I vaguely recognized...

Then the young girl began to move...
She began to walk slowly towards me in the dark blue light.

Something was wrong though... something was not right.
She lifted her arm towards me...
She was sad. Then I saw her neck and the wide, open cut...
She whispered...

Tell him I forgive him...

The roses on her dress curled into bloodstains...
Blood ran from her neck but she began to smile...

I wanted to scream, wanted to awaken...

I sat up; it felt like I was covered in sweat but of course I was not. I was sure I felt cold so I stood up and went to the kitchen to put the kettle on. It was still night and the blue stars were out... not the dark blue of my dream though, which was a relief. A warm caressing light filled the room and relaxed me. There was no moon though... I was still dead and still capable of nightmares.

   I sat with my comforting tea while Arnie slept beside me. It was the early hours of the morning and my afterlife harmony had been shattered.

   I had not been expecting bad dreams... it was a reminder that I was still human.

Whoever this young girl was... wherever that haunting voice had come from, I was sure that I had not seen or heard the last of them.

POST

And I had not. Every night the dream, the nightmare invaded my sleep. It was always the same... the pleading voice, then the young girl I had come to name Rose saying... *Tell him I forgive him...*

Each night the horror seemed to intensify... the girl no longer smiled, she became desperate. The voice became even more frantic and full of fear...

These nightmares were tearing at my soul... they began to question my sanity and I could not allow that. I kept away from The Hillsdown, I needed someone to talk to but I could not burden Jeannette with this. I needed somebody to confide in but I knew that all my close friends were still alive... Steve, Raff, Dickie and Mick; how, I needed to talk to them now. The tormentors of my dreams were at the end of their tether and so was I... then one day a letter arrived.

Arnie alerted me to it, he had always been a good watchdog and his barking indicated that something had arrived through the letterbox. This was a now a new sensation because nobody had ever called on me, no one had ever phoned. My book of contact numbers was completely blank. I was very intrigued when I picked up the letter but also apprehensive. I think that my hand trembled slightly as I opened it. It was addressed simply to Richard. 55 Bridge End, Washington... and in a handwriting style I recognized immediately. I felt tears in my eyes before I started reading...

My dear son Richard,
　I think that it is time for you to see me; your

Acceptance Period is over. Perhaps I should have phoned you but I think that this way is best. There is much for us to talk about. I have started hearing voices in my sleep and I have a feeling that you may have too. Please come over whenever you are ready, I have missed you so much. There is homemade soup waiting for you.

Your loving Mother.

Tears rolled down my cheeks. I touched them and they were real. I reached down and stroked Arnie...

"Come on son, we are going to Ryhope.

I went up stairs and changed into a smart white shirt and black jeans. Then a thought struck me... did I still have a car? Things were more or less how they used to be... how that was I still had no idea. How food was always in the fridge when I required it... fresh milk, a never-ending supply of Guinness? I could not question this too much; surely my head would hurt if I did. I suppose it was all part of the Acceptance Period my mother had mentioned.

I went to the garage and opened the white door... and there it was; my black Fiat Punto looking like it did on the day that I had bought it, a faithful little car that had never let me down. I opened the door and sat inside, I somehow felt complete now that I had wheels to get about. Should I have imagined a Porsche? Why I thought that I don't know but I was happy enough with my old car and that was all that mattered. A quick glance at the petrol gauge indicated that the tank was full and this came as no surprise... did it really need petrol to run on? Again, I was in no mood to dwell on such matters... I was going to see my mother, someone I had not seen for ten years. I called to Arnie and after carefully coaxing him to get in the car we set off.

We were soon heading along the Washington highway towards Shiney Row. Arnie had always been a nervous passenger and it took a while for him to settle down. I still found it funny how he would constantly circle the car floor before curling up into a ball of anxiety. He was an intelligent dog and he knew that riding in cars was dangerous.

As we crossed the river Wear I looked along the beautiful countryside towards South Hylton. It is a hard thing to describe... things looked similar and familiar and yet they were totally different and so it was, all along the country road to Ryhope. Turneresque scenes shifted and shaped before my eyes. The colours were blending and melting as if on a gigantic pallet. It was as if I was hallucinating... it was out of this world.

These distractions though did not take my mind off where I was going. The closer we came to my mother's house the more nervous I became. It was if I had been away for years and I was now returning home... and this in fact was a reality. Apprehension flooded my mind... what if the whole family was there: Uncle Bob, my grandparents... What about great grandparents? Surely not I hoped. Suddenly I was Robert De Niro returning from the Viet Nam war and the music began to play on the radio... I knew that I was not in the right frame of mind for a large family re-union!

I did not have to worry though, I was sure that my mother would be well aware of how delicate my frame of mind might be. She had been a nurse all of her working life and she would know what I would still be going through.

I pulled up outside of her Aged Miners Home on Brick Lane and then took a moment to compose myself. The bungalow was far bigger than I remembered but that was how things were here and I was beginning to get used to it. I walked down the garden path and noticed the wonderful variety of roses that were on display. It reminded me of my own garden... then the little girl Rose from my nightmares entered my thoughts...

"No, not here. Not now."

I was about to knock on the door when it opened and there she stood... shining brown hair and beautiful...

"Hello son, welcome home."

She kissed me on the cheek as I walked into her house but I could not control myself. I turned and hugged her like I would not let go. It felt like my heart was pumping loudly though I knew it was not. Tears welled up in my eyes and I was smiling deliriously. Here was my mother... and she was crying too.

The whole thing was surreal and she was aware of it. She was no longer 75, she looked more than half that age and it almost made me feel like a little boy again. I sat on her soft, flower-patterned sofa and looked to the fireplace. I was immediately aware that the room was at least three times the size I remembered and the furniture and decoration was more or less the same. On the mantelpiece were pictures of my brother and sister and myself. We were all young and we looked happy.

My mother sat down on her favourite chair beside the fire, which was burning gently although there was no heat. Arnie sat gently beside her feet; it was obvious that he had missed her too.

"I have put the kettle on Richard so I will make us both a nice cup of tea in a moment..."

There was a slight silence then she spoke again...

"I... I could not contact you earlier. It is not the way things are done here. Our physical bodies may not be the same but our minds are as delicate as ever."

"It's okay mam I understand."

"Yes, I knew you would. Sometimes people do not.

Their journey through the Portal was probably too harrowing... they do not remember."

She became very thoughtful at this statement but continued...

"They struggle to come to terms with what has happened and where they are..."

She became very sad.

"Look mam, we do not have to discuss all this now. I understand all that you are saying, I am just glad that you are okay and that things are normal."

"Yes, I like that... things are normal."

She suddenly stood and went to the kitchen and then quickly returned with two mugs of tea. My mother's tea always tasted great that is how I remembered it and that is how I imagined it. As we sipped our hot beverage I began to relax. I enquired after uncle Bob, my grandparents and the rest of the family. I said that I was relieved that they were not all here and my mother understood...

"They all live where they used to... where they were happy. Your uncle Bob has his own place now, which is a new farmhouse directly opposite the back of your nanas house. Your granddad built it while he waited for him."

A thought suddenly hit me and mother knew exactly what I was thinking.

"No son, he does not need his walking sticks anymore, that sadness he has left behind."

"I feel so glad for him... when can I go and see him?"

"Let us have some soup first... we still have to talk about those voices."

She stood up again and went to the kitchen. This statement slightly dampened things but she was just being a mother. I needed help and advice and she knew it.

Mother came back with two small trays and the piping hot soup. The smell of the soup could not be just a memory, it had to be real and the soup was delicious even though I knew it was probably tasteless. I was about to ask my mother how this could be so but then declined and carried on enjoying my meal.

When we finished our lunch I decided to talk about the dreams...

"You say that you have heard the voices mam?"

"Yes... yes I have."

She paused for a moment and looked pensive...

"...It is your son JJ."

"What..."

This came as a shock but deep down inside I knew it to be true.

"The wisdom of the Blue Veins has decided to deliver his prayers to you. Your son is in great turmoil..."

I began to feel unwell. I strangely remembered that I had not been physically sick for about twelve years or so and was determined not to spoil that.

"Blue Veins? What are they?"

"Do not worry yourself about this too much son, you will come to understand things better later. They are simply our connection with the Clear Conscious."

"Clear Conscious?"

My mother knew that this was becoming too much for me and went silent. I shook my head.

"So I am receiving messages? Echoes?"

"Yes Richard, JJ is disturbed. He is praying for your help!"

"...And the little girl I call Rose, who is she?"

My mother looked concerned with this statement...

"Rose? Who is she?"

"You have heard the voices..."

"Yes... he is my grandson."

"But you have not seen the girl?"

"No, I know of no girl called Rose."

I felt the blood drain from my cheeks and this prompted my mother to go and pour two large gins for us...

"Here son, this may help."

"Thanks mam, I'm sure it will."

I drank the gin in one go then described the young girl to her. I omitted the gruesome part... the part that indicated that she had obviously been murdered. I did not like where this was taking me. Surely JJ was not to blame for this young girls death! Perhaps there had been some sort of an accident... *TELL HIM I FORGIVE HIM* echoed ominously in my mind. I did not tell mother about what the girl had said.

My mother sipped at her drink thoughtfully then said...

"This Rose is just confused... she is what we call a 'lost soul.' She has not settled in this realm because her passing through the Portal has been too traumatic for her. She probably does not remember who she is; she drifts and accesses our thoughts looking for somebody she knows, someone she recognizes... Perhaps she used to live near you?"

This was highly plausible, Devils Wood was nearby but why would she tell me that *HE WAS FORGIVEN*?

My mother had seemingly turned into some sort of a Medium and I found this almost funny but I realized that this it was an understanding gained by experience. I thought about what she had said but concluded that she was wrong.

"No mam, I do not think that she is lost or has forgotten who she is... I think she is a messenger!"

We both fell silent after I had said this and I waited for mother to finish her drink. I knew what I had to try and do...

"I need to go back mam. I mean; can I go back... is that even possible? I need to know what has happened... JJ needs my help, no matter what he has done!"

This suddenly prompted questions about my death...

"And me? What happened to me? I was fit and healthy..."

"I do not know son. All I know is that we were informed that you had entered the Portal. The Clear Conscious is gracious like that; they give us time to prepare. Your father Charles met you..."

"So it was dad then, in the white BMW."

Mother seemed amused by this...

"BMW... is that what he is driving these days, hah! he must have finally had some luck on the horses."

"He did not say who he was."

"No and you know why now."

"Yes... he looked so young. I was near Castletown... for some reason."

My thoughts drifted for a moment, trying to remember... but nothing came to mind, I was not ready to recall. Mother broke my muse...

"Well, your father still lives in Pennywell near his beloved club..."

Pennywell! It hit me like a bolt of lightning. I still had friends living there... then I suddenly remembered my childhood dog Bengo and again I had to fight back tears. He was dog made from the same mould as Arnie, but a cross between a boxer and whippet. Strong, fast and intelligent... we had so many adventures together... I knew I was drifting again then mother continued...

"...Your father and I meet up now and then and have spoken about getting back together again... but maybe not just yet."

I was still thinking of Bengo and my long lost childhood...

"That would make me so happy mam... you both were so lonely for so long."

"Oh we are not so lonely... Your father has his family and friends and I have mine."

My mother went thoughtful for a moment then she continued...

"You asked about being able to return. It is possible I think; spirits do walk the Earth. I do not recommend it though... it is too early for you!

And I... I am not really sure how it is achieved."

This broke my nostalgic spell and refocused my commitment to my son...

"I must try mam, I cannot ignore JJ's plea for help... he is my son! Surely these Blue Veins have brought me his words and sorrow for a reason. You must know someone who can advise me."

My mother looked sternly into my eyes...

"Your grandfather... if anyone knows what to do, it will be him. He answered what questions he could when I arrived here; perhaps he can answer yours. Come, fetch Arnie and we will take a walk to see him."

Chapter Five

RYHOPE CHURCH

We left my mothers house by the back door and then turned left onto the track way that lead to the back of my grandfathers house which was situated on Burdon Avenue. Arnie seemed to remember where he was and frantically began to run around searching for long forgotten scents. There was a feeling of a summers walk about it as we past the Ryhope Colliery Welfare football ground where I had played many games for Sunderland Schoolboys. Memories began to flood back again...

"I see that you remember the football ground Richard."

"How could I not; I remember that my uncle Bob was allowed to watch my matches for Sunderland boys in his light blue Tri-car. Does he still have it?" I enquired. This was a car used by many disabled people at the time. I remembered that he used to visit us regularly when we lived in Pennywell. I swear that my dog Bengo could hear that car coming from miles away and his wagging tail and enthusiastic barking always alerted us to uncle Bob's imminent arrival.

Mother gave a short laugh...

"Funnily enough he still does. I think he keeps it for sentimental reasons."

It was literally only a five-minute walk to my grandfathers back garden. Again everything was familiar and bigger, the only thing that was really different was the farmhouse directly opposite. My grandfather had done a great job on the building and obviously made my uncle Bob proud. Previously there had only been wide rolling cornfields where the new farmhouse was situated and these had been owned by the farm next to the football ground. Now there was this magnificent farmhouse that was complete with barns, garages and stables. It was as if my grandfather had won the lottery. I stopped and stared at it for a moment but I could not see my favourite uncle anywhere.

"Lovely isn't it. Bob calls it The Ranch; you know how he loved his Cowboy films. It shows you what is capable here in the Promised Land when you put your mind to it. You could build a house right next to it if you wanted...?"

"Could I? What about land rights..."

"I know that this will be hard to get used to but money is no longer a relevant commodity. The land is ever changeable and flexible. Nobody owns the land anymore, there are no more arguments, and there is no more greed. Come and live beside us."

"Yes, I think I will... although it is a bit far from Fatfield."

"Fatfield?"

"I'll tell you later."

We walked down the garden path that immediately made me feel young again. There were no flowers in this garden, only vegetables of every variety...

"You can see why my soup is still the best in the world, eh son?"

Before we entered the back door; a large shaggy haired dog whose breed I did not recognize greeted us. It barked a few times at Arnie but he did not take this as a threat and the two dogs then began to playfully run around the garden.

As we entered the kitchen, delicious, familiar cooking smells assailed my nose that again set nostalgic memories in motion. My grandparents and my uncle Bob were waiting for us... nana and granddad looking like they had just stepped out of the lovely framed portraits I had of them that were painted when they were young. My uncle looking more like my grandfathers brother than his son; was sitting on his large wooden chair beside the old woollen sock machine that he used to make a living from. None of my football kits were ever complete without a pair of uncle Bob's sports socks! Looking at my uncle and the odd machine made me feel like I had stepped back in time. He stood up and I noticed immediately how much stronger he looked. He walked proudly towards me without the use of walking sticks then took my hand and shook it firmly...

"Hello son. You are home now with your family."

He was obviously much taller and younger than he used to be and was completely different to how I remembered him. He was now the man he would have been had he not been so terribly afflicted by rheumatoid arthritis as a young boy.

"I am not the man I was, am I?" he said and laughed a little at this. Then my grandmother spoke...

"Come son, come Bess, sit at the table. Dick, get us all a drink."

"Aye, good idea Dorothy."

My mother and I sat at the large kitchen table beside the window, while my grandfather went to the front room. My uncle Bob stood in front of the old farmhouse oven, which as ever had something cooking in it. Granddad came back with a large bottle of brandy and poured us all a large glassful. He lifted his glass...

"Here's to Richard and his rebirth. Thank God he has made it through the Portal safely."

Everybody lifted their glasses and then took a drink but as I sipped my soothing brandy, my grandfather's last sentence began to hit home.

My mother spoke next and came straight to the

point; she never was one for small talk...

"Richard has a problem I'm afraid. I've never mentioned it to you before but now the time is right and we've come for your advice."

This surprised my grandparents and uncle Bob; I could tell that this was something that they were not expecting.

My grandfather was quick to respond...

"Problem Bess? But he looks fine. We know how the Portal can be traumatic depending on the circumstances..."

"Oh yes, I'm okay... it's just..." I quickly intervened but I became nervous and began to stutter. My mother took over and explained my dilemma to them...

"Richard has been beset by voices... prayers from his youngest son asking for help. I have heard them too and they are heartfelt."

There was silence in the kitchen; I sensed that they immediately knew that this was serious. My grandfather spoke up and broke everybody's thoughts...

"The Clear Conscious has brought you his prayers for a reason."

"Yes granddad, I must go back. I must try and help him somehow."

Grandfather topped up everyone's drinks so that our glasses were all full. There was a serious look on his face...

"I don't know of anyone that has returned Richard. I have heard that it is possible but I imagine that it must be very dangerous. Do you want to take that chance son?"

My answer was simple... "I must!"

My grandfather finished his drink in one go and placed his glass down on the table...

"We must go to the church then and see the Reverend. He is the man to talk to. Bessie, you stop here with your mother. Bob you go and hitch up Mustard.

"Mustard?" The name puzzled me and mother had the answer...

"Your grandfathers horse Richard, worked with him for years for the Store. You must have been too young to remember..."

"Horse? Are you joking? I can go and get my car," I said but my grandfather was adamant.

"I don't trust cars, don't like them. Mustard takes me everywhere like he has always done."

There was no point arguing as uncle Bob went straight away to get the horse and... cart? I hoped not.

We all waited in the vegetable garden and soon uncle Bob returned with a magnificent white horse with a golden mane, pulling a small buggy behind it.

"Get in Richard, your carriage awaits you," said uncle Bob with a wry smile on his face. My grandfather and I climbed up into the buggy and we set off at a brisk pace. I waved back to my mother, who was holding Arnie as we trotted away down the back lane. I had to admit that I immediately began enjoy the ride, proof then I thought that life here held many new possibilities and new experiences... but I still had no idea of what was waiting just around the corner. I was soon to be thrown into a sequence of events that were simply unbelievable... a personal ordeal that would defy description but an ordeal I would have to endure!

Ryhope Church was at the bottom of the main street, past a wide variety of shops, pubs and bookies. I think Ryhope even beat Fatfield for the number of pubs and clubs on one road. I was also aware that we were not the only ones using good old horsepower; in the distance I spotted coal merchants delivering to houses in the time-honoured tradition. I swear I could feel a breeze through my hair as we cantered at a quick pace down the steep winding road to the church. It did not take us long to get there.

Uncle Bob pulled Mustard off the main road, onto a grass embankment next to the church. St. Paul's stood on a slight hill in a picturesque part of the village and was surrounded by high brick walls and occasional trees. It was nice to feel that the old church was still important to its immediate society.

I knew that the church had been built in 1870 and that its unusual features were the pyramidal roof of the tower and the fact that the brick walls surrounding it were made from the stone sleepers from the colliery railway. This information had not been gained from Google but from a quaint old book called 'Ryhope in Picture Cards,' given to me by my uncle Bob when we were alive. The church seemed compact and sturdy with the tower being central and quite imposing. Beautiful flowerbeds surrounded it and two tall trees stood either side of the entrance. I remembered that I had painted a picture of the church a few years ago in my own expressionist style and I had poetically included the graves of my family and myself although I knew that they were really buried in Ryhope Cemetery. This memory brought a chill to me as I remembered that I had bought the plot behind my mother's grave for myself. This posed an unusual dilemma for me… could I really go and look at my own grave? This thought sickened me slightly but I decided that I should.

As we walked past the two trees up towards the church, I asked my grandfather whom it was we were going to see.

"The vicar of this Parish is called Reverend Wilson, the original vicar who raised the funds to build the church."

"Will he be here now?"

"This was his life and his work. If he is not here, then he will be not too far away."

As we entered the church I immediately felt an eerie sensation... echoes of people talking and praying gently permeated my head. Then I heard music I recognized immediately, Brian Eno's Complex Heaven floated ominously over the voices that were now tinged with sadness. I had attended services here; the christening of my son Robert, the memorial service for my mother but I somehow knew that these ambient sounds were from my own funeral!

Uncle Bob seemed to realize what I was experiencing...

"Do not worry son, you will get used to it... the memory will eventually fade."

We walked down the main aisle towards the Altar and my grandfather was right, Reverend Wilson was indeed here. He was a tall man of retirement age with shining grey hair and a placid countenance; he turned towards us...

"Ah Dick, Robert, it is good to see you both... and who is this with you?"

"This is my grandson Richard, Reverend... the reason we have come to talk to you."

The vicar motioned to the left of him "Come, let us sit in the garden. I feel you are troubled somewhat."

We walked with him to the right of the Altar, through a side door that led to the outside grounds.

We sat at a large wooden table that looked as old as the church itself and for a moment we enjoyed the view. From the high point where the church was situated, we looked out towards the North Sea.

"Beautiful isn't it..." said Reverend Wilson. "It is a sight I never sicken of."

We looked down to the green cliff edges that

towered over the soft sandy beaches beneath them. It was a tranquil scene as many species of seagulls glided serenely over the calm blue waves...

"It would be nice to have a stormy setting now and then though," added the Reverend thoughtfully. Then he looked to us and especially to me...

"Now then, how can I help you?"

There was a moment of hesitation; then I recounted the dream of the girl and the pain of my son's prayers to the vicar. My grandfather and my uncle were not aware of the young girl and this clearly intrigued them. Reverend Wilson sat silent for awhile, then chose his words carefully...

"I think that your mother is right. This girl is a lost soul and has not settled. She drifts between the two realities. I fear that she may have been murdered and is still being preyed upon by the Dark Conscious..."

The Reverend looked me squarely in the eye... I knew that he was thinking the worst.

"But her message Reverend, what does it mean..."
"The Clear Conscious is trying to help her... but we must not jump to conclusions. Your son is praying for help but we must not assume that both are connected. It may be pure coincidence... or perhaps some terrible accident..."

Everyone fell silent; a sense of frustration filled the air... I broke the tension...

"You can see why I have to know what has happened then. My son is a good man. He has had troubles in his life like everyone else but I know that he would never ever consider such a thing as..."

I began to stutter as the words gagged in my mouth and I began to shake as an acute depression gripped me...

"I... I have to go back. Please help me Reverend, tell me I can... tell me how I can!" I was fighting back tears as my uncle put his hand on my shoulder to comfort me.

Again the garden became silent, like the stony graves that were laid all around us. Then the Reverend spoke...

"It is possible to go back Richard but only if the Clear Conscious allows it. The danger is great though and to my knowledge only one person from my Parish has been back and I am afraid that he is now a resident of Cherry Knowles Hospital. He has paid a terrible price..."

This statement shocked me on many levels...

"You are telling me that there are patients in Cherry Knowles?"

"Of course son, you should know by now that the passage through the Portal can be dangerous. The Dark Conscious inhabits these corridors and will try and claim your soul. Sometimes they almost succeed..."

"Could I... speak to this person?"

I could tell that my grandfather and uncle agreed with this. They knew that I should see the reality of what could happen for myself.

"His name is William Shields and I visit him regularly. Sometimes he is coherent; sometimes he seems to be lost in terrible memories. He has never said why he went back or what happened but what I know is that this experience has scarred him severely. William served his country in World War II; I know that he is a man of stern stuff. He is not somebody who would buckle easily; whatever happened has proven costly. The Clear Conscious is trying to heal him but it is a long process, I am sure though that they comfort him in his darkest moments."

"Can we Reverend.... Can we go and see him?"

The vicar looked to my grandfather...

"I think we should Dick. Your grandson should see

what could befall him. Our old world is a battleground, a war is being fought that is perhaps being lost... maybe we need more Angels!"

CHERRY KNOWLES

We left the garden and walked back down to Mustard who was happily chomping away on the grass beside the church walls. The hospital was not far away, ten minutes or so along the Stockton road. I remembered that my cousin David Pirum had started his working life there as a male nurse and I also recalled that my father had spent a short spell there to treat a slight drinking problem he had. The story about how he checked himself out when they had suggested that electric shock treatment would cure him, never failed to make me smile.

As we approached the main doors, I noticed that the hospital was more or less how I remembered it from years ago, an interlocking series of long flat buildings. All was quiet and peaceful; there was a feeling of a monk's monastery about the place as we entered the quiet reception area. The hospital seemed empty; it was like being on board a ghost ship. It was obvious that there were not that many patients in residence. We walked down a long pristine corridor, and then turned left into a series of larger long-term residential apartments. The Reverend stopped outside room 5...

"This is the one... various family members and the volunteers that run the hospital care for William here. I think you may have guessed that there are not that many patients here, most recover quickly and I look forward to the day when William is confident enough to leave."

The Reverend knocked quietly on Williams door...

"William, it is Reverend Wilson and some friends of

mine. Can we come in?"

A confident robust voice called from inside…

"Why aye Reverend, you know the door is never locked."

We walked into the room and I was pleasantly surprised to find that William's apartment was more like an elegant up market hotel residence than some clinical hospital abode. We stood in a large room that had double doors that were open to the hospital gardens. William came to greet us and it was obvious that he was in good spirits as he shook all of our hands.

"Good to see you Reverend Wilson and who have you brought to see me then?"

"This is Dick Pirum, his son Robert and his grandson Richard. They asked if they could come and talk to you if that is okay?"

"Of course it is, I have been feeling much better lately… my dreams of little Rosie have been pleasant lately. Memories of happier days…"

William seemed distant for a moment; then he slowly walked towards the double doors.

We found ourselves glancing nervously at each other, the shock of hearing Rose's name astonished us. I wanted to ask William about her but the Reverend held my arm firmly…

"No Richard, not yet… this is highly unusual. I have never heard him mention this girls name before. It could be a sign that his full recovery is imminent."

"But Reverend, what if he has been having the same dream… surely he knows what has befallen her…. And what of my son JJ? What has he to do with all this?"

"I think Richard, that you should not mention your dreams… not even that you intend to return. Come, let us join him in the garden."

William was sitting at an ornately decorated table and we all joined him in the relaxing setting. I looked around the hospital garden and felt that I was sitting in a five star hotel that was complete with tennis courts and a swimming pool.

"I love it here and you can see why... but I'd much rather be at home" said William "I feel sorry that I have caused my family so much grief."

William was a small, stocky man with a face that was full of character... I began to wonder about what he had been through before ending up here. I sensed he was still troubled and lonely... a man who was missing his family.

"Nonsense..." said Reverend Wilson. "You have not been well William, your family is proud of you and rightly so."

Again, William became thoughtful...

"Each day I feel stronger..." he said, then suddenly turned to us...

"I was allowed to go back you know... the Clear Conscious gave me their blessing."

A slight breeze picked up in the garden but none of us noticed this change in the weather, we were totally absorbed in what William was saying...

"But I paid the price... I could not defeat him."

"Defeat him?" I blurted out. "Defeat who?"

Again the Reverend held my arm as a visible change came over William. He suddenly seemed sad and broken; in an instant he was a different man. He looked at me with darker eyes.

"I'm sorry son, I cannot say any more... maybe one day..."

William concentration was beginning to waver; I had to interrupt...

"And Rosie William, who is Rosie?"

This brought lightness back to his face and a defiant mood...

"Rosie is my granddaughter!"

This shocked me so much that I fell silent.

Reverend Wilson was quick to intervene...

"You have never mentioned Rosie before William, neither have your family?"

"Yes, I know Reverend but I have been having dreams lately... not nightmares."

This was too much for me and my grandfather and uncle knew it. I had to ask the question...

"Why William, why did you go back?"

Suddenly that gentle breeze became a stiff cold wind... the weather was changing quickly and I could tell that this concerned everyone but William. Ever since I had arrived in this afterlife the climate had always been consistent... something ominous was happening. We all felt apprehensive as heavy dark clouds rolled slowly towards us. The blue light in the garden changed slowly to a Halloween green and a sense of danger filled the air... something or someone was approaching...

Beside the pool he walked...
A small man in a white coat...
Sickly smile and dirty hair...
A storm followed him.
Distant rumbling....
We sat and stared in disbelief.
This was no dream...
This was happening...

Closer he came...
Shifty eyes... bloodshot eyes...
A thin face... a pointy nose.

We could see that he was evil...
Smell that he was evil...

Nosferatu walked towards us...

Suddenly Reverend Wilson stood up and held his hand out towards the hideous apparition...

"Be gone vile creature... be gone from this place of peace!"

Bram Stoker, Hammer, filled my head... I felt like laughing hysterically but I could not. The stench of evil was all around us...

Nosferatu looked viciously towards the vicar... a low laughter came from him as he swirled around to look at us... but the Reverend persisted...

"You are not welcome here whoever you are, again I say be gone!"

The sordid snigger slowly dissolved as the unwelcome vision faded...

Nosferatu left us and we all breathed heavy sighs of relief.

We then turned and looked to William who was slumped back in his chair, eyes heavy and closed. Reverend Wilson looked at our shaken faces...

"It was Williams memory... never has he shown so much, usually it is just darkness and shadows."

"But how?" I enquired.

"Heaven is made of memories Richard, that is something you will come to understand," replied Reverend Wilson.

"So this is Heaven then Reverend?"

He looked at me with compassionate eyes...

"This is our Heaven Richard and that is all that matters."

The weather slowly changed back to what it had been and a bright calmness filled the garden once again. William was peaceful too and now there was a caring nurse beside him. Then an amazing thing happened, something I will never forget... iridescent blue tendrils descended softly from above and attached themselves gently to William's upper body. For a moment he looked like a shimmering life-size puppet and a warm smile filled his face...

"What the..." I could tell that even my grandfather had never seen anything like this before but the Reverend obviously had...

"Do not be afraid my friends, they are simply the Blue Veins of the Clear Conscious... we are honoured that we have been allowed to see them!"

The vicar knew that it was now time for us to go...

"I think that we should leave William now" he said and the nurse nodded in agreement. Just as we were about to leave the garden though, William's eyes slowly opened and he spoke directly to me...

"I know that you are thinking of returning son, I know also that you are a Slider like myself! I sensed it the moment I held your hand."

I had felt it too, a slight tingling as we had shaken hands. William's face was now deadly serious as he continued...

"This is good; your electrical energy will make you stronger when you have made it back... Beware the Portal though! The journey will not be easy! They will try and deceive you and claim you. They will think that you are an Angel, soft and easy to kill..."

William's eyes turned to the skies for a moment; then he continued...

"You will feel mortal again... and mortals can die! Remember that your soul can be lost forever; if you are killed you will be nothing... you will cease to exist!"

These words sent a chill down my spine. I felt the hairs on my arm prickle but this was no acted warning in some horror movie, this was real! I was speechless; I did not know what to say... I had been warned! The Reverend spoke graciously for me...

"Thank you for the advice William, I am sure that Richard is very grateful. I will call again soon. God bless."

We left the room and returned to Mustard.

We sat in silence as we took Reverend Wilson back to Ryhope church. No-one mentioned William's vision, surely it was one man's memory that was best forgotten. After we had stopped outside the entrance to the church, the vicar stepped carefully from the buggy...

"I hope that has been helpful my friends... you now know the dangers involved. I do not know what that apparition was but I had to confront it."

Strangely, the small ghostly man was somehow familiar to me but I could not recall why. A last pressing question dismissed him from my mind...

"There is still one thing I do not know Reverend... How do I access a Portal?"

The vicar simply smiled at this question...

"I said earlier that I knew it was possible. The answer to your question is obvious... Portals open where people die! Hospitals; care homes, places of tragedy... You will be able to pass through them but that is only if the Clear Conscious allows it! I am sure that your passage has been approved so go with God my son and remember, if you need someone to talk to... this church is always here. God bless, I will pray for you."

Reverend Wilson then turned slowly and began to walk towards the church. Uncle Bob motioned to Mustard and we set off up Ryhope road towards our waiting family.

My uncle took Mustard to his stable while my grandfather and I went to relate the news. My mother and grandmother sat patiently as my grandfather told them everything that had happened. Mother became restless and agitated; she stood up and paced nervously around the kitchen...

"You should not do this son... you may end up like William or worse! He might spend an eternity in Cherry Knowles!"

I tried to lighten the mood...

"Well that would not be so bad, it is like The Ritz up there now!"

My grandfather chuckled at this but mother remained serious, I continued quickly...

"William is recovering mam, we could tell..."

"But what he said... the dangers. You could be lost to us forever!"

"That's not going to happen mam. I'm a big boy now, I can take care off myself..."

At that point uncle Bob returned from his farmhouse; he had heard what had been said...

"It's no use Bess, he's made his mind up. All we can do now is pray for him!"

My uncle knew that I was eager to be on my way...

"Well everyone, I must go now and prepare. Are you coming along mam?"

My mother was sad and I hoped that she would stay awhile with her family.

"No... I want to stay here a bit longer..."

I hugged her tightly and whispered "Don't worry, everything will be fine. I will be back in no time." I hugged everybody else then looked around for Arnie. My uncle knew where he was...

"They're in the cornfields playing, I heard them barking."

We all walked into the vegetable garden and I called for my dog. The two dogs came running back at once and were happy to see us.

"Come on son, we're leaving now."

I kissed mother gently on the cheek then I started to walk with Arnie back to the car. I knew that they were all watching but I could not look back.

PENNYWELL

There was something I had to do first before I went to the hospital and the Portal, I had to see my father. My mother had said that he still lived in Portrush Road, so I drove quickly through Silksworth and Farringdon towards Pennywell. I passed the Round Robin which no longer seemed the same pub I remembered, then continued into Ford estate where I turned left to head towards where I used to live.

It was no longer the Pennywell I remembered. The Quarry and the Big Field had been housed over but my old junior school Quarry View remained, which was heartening. I turned left at the school, then second right into Portrush Road. A million memories began to bombard me but I had to focus, I did not have time to be sentimental. I pulled up beside the house of my childhood and walked with Arnie to the front door.

I was surprised to see that the door was still painted yellow but the house was now detached and much larger than it ever was. I looked around at the rest of the street, which seemed a lot longer and more affluent. There was no sign of any neighbours though, no children playing on the road... I was getting nostalgic again. I knocked loudly on the door... which triggered barking from the back of the house. I looked to the side door, which I knew led to the old washhouse and back garden. The door was open and I immediately recognized the bark...

A low growl came from beside the washhouse... I knew that it was the dog I had loved as a boy; it was Bengo! He emerged slowly from the doorway and it was obvious that he did not recognize me at first; he seemed to be more concerned with Arnie violating his territory. Arnie began to growl too but I suspected this was one fight he might not win. Bengo had been a cross between a whippet and a boxer. He had never lost one dogfight in Pennywell and there had been some vicious, starving dogs in those days. He was not a malicious dog though; just a loner... that was capable of seeing whole packs of dogs off without any help. He had been the perfect, protective companion for me, on what had sometimes been a bit of a rough housing estate. Right now though he was being a guard dog...

"Hey son, it's me... don't you remember?"

I reached out my hand and he stopped growling. Arnie wisely stood behind me although he was ready to protect against this formidable opponent.

Bengo's eyes softened... he slowly began to realize who I was and his tail began to wag. He came towards me and licked my face like he was a young puppy again. I could swear that there were not only tears in my eyes but in the eyes of the two dogs too!

As I had with Arnie I hugged my long lost dog and patted his solid, hard body. One thing was for sure though; he had not softened any. He then approached Arnie and barked at him; only this time it was not a warning, it was a welcome. Arnie simply wagged his tail in approval...

"This is Arnie boy... now then, where is my dad?"

This was a stupid question, as I knew exactly where he would be if he were not at home. I turned to Arnie and hoped that he would understand...

"I am going to the Ford and Hylton Club Arnie, you stay here with Bengo okay." Arnie barked loudly twice at me then followed Bengo into the back garden. I was happy that the two dogs were together... I thought about the two other dogs I had owned in my lifetime.

Solo had only been a puppy when he had been killed by a hit and run driver, in front of my eyes on this very street. I wondered where he was. Then I thought of the dog I had bought from Battersea Dogs Home, when I was an art student in London. Speedo had lived to be eighteen years old and I assumed that he could be waiting for me at my old house in Ayton. I decided that I would look for him when I returned from my... mission? This thought made me pause a moment... is that what it was then? The truth was I had no idea what it was; all I knew was that it was something I had to do... I had to try and help my son. I got back into the car and drove to the Club.

Like the Round Robin, the Club looked like it had been renovated on a grand scale. My last memory of this place was of a boarded up, run down hovel that had probably been closed by the Police because of its history of violence and drugs. It had become a symbol for the gradual social decline of certain parts of the estate over the years. Which was sad as the Club had been quite a social attraction in its heyday. For my father, the Club had been his local...he remembered the good times spent there and remained faithful to it until the very end.

There was still a sixties look about the place which I thought was quite cool and the name The Club was lit up in a neon Hollywood style above the main doors. Even though the frontage was now quite inviting I knew that inside there was still likely to be a variety of hardened characters enjoying a drink.

I parked my Fiat Punto in the large car park to the right of the Club and walked briskly to the entrance. Before I could enter though, there was still a man at the reception box window who enquired if I was a member or not. I told him that my club membership had probably expired but my father Charlie was a member.

"Charlie? Why didn't you say man? You'll find him in the bar son."

It was amusing that someone was calling me 'son' when he looked a similar age to me, although he did have a fifties rock and roll hairstyle that was just dripping with thick shiny Brylcreem.

Inside, the format of the building seemed more or less as it used to be. Straight ahead was the 'posh' lounge and to the right was the concert room where many a 'turn' had died a swift death. Upstairs were the snooker room and function rooms and to my immediate left was the bar... where women were strictly not allowed! I did seem to recall that two brave women had tried to sit and have a drink in the bar but were loudly booed by the men resulting in a quick exit. I do not think any other women ever tried again.

I walked into the bright, spacious room and looked around. Older looking men were sitting playing cards and dominoes along the tables in front of the wide-open windows. It was a scene full of well built men who were smoking and drinking heavily, laughing and swearing. The Club may have had a classier look to it now but inside the bar, it was still like the old Wild West.

At the far end of the bar stood a group of younger men who were playing darts. Standing beside them drinking a bottle of Double Maxim was... my father.

I stood for a moment and looked at him. It was the same young looking man that had driven me home in his BMW. He was smartly dressed in a white shirt and a blue tie; one thing he always insisted on wearing when he went to the Club. I knew that this was another surreal situation, though I was aware that I was beginning to get used to such things. I walked over to him and patted him firmly on the back...

"Hello dad... thanks for the lift home."

He turned at once but he was not as surprised as I thought he might be.

"Hello son, I was wondering when you might turn up… can I get you a pint?"

"I'll have a Guinness please dad."

"A Guinness? What's wrong with a good old bottle of Vauxies"

"I've been drinking the black stuff for years now… millions of drunken Irishmen can't be that wrong eh?"

My father smiled at my astute observation and ordered the round.

Father had been talking to a man who I assumed to be of a similar age as he too wore a smart tie. I was introduced to him…

"Jack, this is my youngest son Richard."

I shook the man's hand then quickly enquired…

"Uncle Jack?"

"No, no son he still resides somewhere in Birmingham. This is Jacky Ness who I used to work with. Now if you will excuse us Jack, I'll have a sit down with my son."

We picked up our pints and took a table in the corner beside one of the long windows. The view from where I sat was of the Big Field, which I fondly remembered was more commonly known as The Blackie. This was the top of the field and there were still no houses on it yet. Father noticed me gazing at it…

"Sometimes buildings spring up on it over night, quite amazing really. It is always a mystery to me how it never gets overcrowded though" he said as he took a sip of his beloved beer.

"Yes, I've been thinking about that. I think it has something to do with overlapping realities…"

"Overlapping realities? Hey you're drinking in the Ford and Hylton Club son, not Durham University…"

I laughed out loudly as I looked outside at a serene Pennywell...

"The old estate has brushed up well dad, don't you think. Perhaps it should be renamed New Pennywell?"

"New Pennywell? ...Yeah, I like the sound of that. Don't be too deceived though there is still the odd bout of fisticuffs around here now and then." This he said with a mischievous glint in his eye and I suddenly remembered again that my father had been a boxing champion in the Army, during the War. He had been a Sergeant but had unfortunately lost a stripe for using his boxing skills in too many pub brawls.

There was a moment's silence between us as we sat enjoying our drinks. I guess when there is so much to say you sometimes don't know where to start. Then my father looked to me and enquired...

"So, are you going to stop awhile and have a few pints with your old man then?"

This I knew would be a very long session but I did not have the time...

"I can't stop too long dad... I... I've decided to go back."

"Go back? Go back where? ...South Africa? London?"

"No dad, back to my two sons."

There was an immediate puzzled look in his eyes...

"Two sons?"

Of course... there was no way he could have known as he had died before they were born.

"Yes, I have two sons just like yourself but... one of them is in trouble. That is why I am going back!"

Fathers amicable face froze, then a serious frown came over it...

"You can't go back son... surely it is too dangerous. Why are you considering this?"

I related the story of Rose and JJ's prayers to him

and he became deeply thoughtful... a lady from the bar brought us more beer.

"You know son when I was in Burma, I was blown up by a grenade and shot in the foot... remember that limp I used to have? Well, something else happened in that damned jungle. Something that I have never mentioned to anybody, not even your mother. I did write it all down though and hid it in the loft, come to think of it the manuscript will probably still be there."

He paused for a moment and I knew that he was reminiscing...

"You remember that I spent a short spell in Cherry Knowles son a long, long time ago?"

"Yes dad... I've just come from there."

This puzzled him slightly but he continued...

"That episode was primarily down to what happened to me in Burma."

"Which was?"

"I won't tell you the whole story... only that I was saved by someone in that jungle, someone who may have been an... Angel! ...And you know what I... I saved him!"

Father's eyes glazed over and his face darkened suddenly, I could tell that he was back there in Burma. I hoped that his memory would not materialize like Williams; I don't think I would have been able to stand it. It was happening though... I looked out to the Big Field where the light of the sky had changed to a burning yellow; I thought that I could even see the outline of the sun through the searing haze. I watched in amazement as a dense, green foliage began to creep menacingly over the grass towards us. I frantically hoped that my father's memory would not reach the Club... and luckily it did not.

Father snapped out of his trance and the distant vision faded...

"What I really want to tell you Richard is that our souls were nearly lost that day. It was our greatest test and had we failed to endure, I would not be here right now enjoying a drink with you. Do not go back son, please!"

He was really concerned for me but that was the point, I was concerned for my son and told him so. After that, he knew how committed I was...

"I just thought that I would come and see you before I go" I said and explained that I had been to see Reverend Wilson about how to return.

I finished my pint and stood up...

"I've left my dog Arnie with Bengo dad if that's okay? I'm sure they'll be alright together until I get back."

"Sure son, I'll watch them both for you..."

"Okay then, I'll be on my way..."

"Remember son, it will probably be winter; you might need to wear something warm eh? I'm not sure how it all works..."

"Good thinking dad, you sound just like me mam..." I jokingly replied.

Then he became extremely serious...

"That evil... that was in the jungle. It will be here in Sunderland when you return... I am sure!"

I hugged him gently; then left the bar. I decided to take his advice and go and get my leather jacket before I went to the hospital.

As I drove back to Washington, I could not get my fathers last words out of my mind...

"THAT EVIL... THAT EVIL WILL BE HERE, IN SUNDERLAND!"

Chapter Six

PORTAL

I did go and get my black leather jacket, I also thought a blue denim shirt, black jeans and my steel toe Doctor Martin shoes might come in handy too. Standing in my bedroom I wondered what else I might need... sunglasses for some reason, even though it was probably wintertime. Mind you, Washington did somehow get its fair share of sunlight I seemed to remember. Now what else would I need? Perhaps I would need fresh underwear? Now things were really getting silly as I stupidly began to think about packing a suitcase! ...I was nervous and I knew it and this was going to be no holiday! The song Travellin' Light by J.J. Cale came to mind and I pulled myself together, I wanted to get this over as soon as possible so I left the house at once and drove to Sunderland General Hospital.

I parked directly opposite the main doors and looked to the sky. It was dark now and the bright blue stars cast a caring glow over the hospital. I did not get out of the car immediately as a cloud of doubt had cast a shadow over me.

"What the hell am I doing?" I asked myself...

"I must be mad! ...This could be the end of me, forever!"

The longer I sat there in the visitors car-park, the more I was convinced that I was going to turn the ignition and drive back home... back to what though? More nightmares, more heart wrenching pleas for help? I knew that I would not survive that mentally and that I could not allow! Had I ever been scared of my responsibilities? To my work and my sons?

No... and I would not start now! I puffed out my chest, opened the car door and walked to the hospital entrance. My life in death was about to change...

Like Cherry Knowles, Sunderland hospital felt practically deserted but again this was obviously understandable. I looked for the Intensive Care ward and proceeded quickly to it. Lonely corridors and stairways made me walk with caution, as there is definitely something spooky about an empty hospital. Then as I passed one particular wardroom that made me stop dead in my tracks! ...I knew this room. I imagined the smell... bright flowers, clean bed linen and medication. It was the room my mother had died in!

A cold sadness filled me; then a memory came back to me like a bolt of lightning striking my mind...

The face from William's nightmare...

The face from my nightmare...

A face from long ago...

It was the hospital porter from that terrible night.

Grief can cripple you and I stood there shaking, even though I knew my mother was now safe and with her family. It was the sudden recall of what the porter had done in my dream that was making me quiver. I felt sickened and vengeful... then I heard Reverend Wilson's voice call out...

"Be gone vile creature, be gone from this place!"

Immediately the porters face faded from my mind and I was alone again on the quiet ward.

I walked onto the next room and was surprised to see that there were people inside. Two women and a man sat beside an empty bed in silence. One of the women noticed me and smiled. It was as if they were waiting for something, their faces were calm and peaceful. I then realized what they were waiting for... the arrival of a loved one!

I slowly entered the room but they did not look to me, I assumed that they simply thought that I too knew the person that was soon to appear. I was sure that as far as they were concerned, the Clear Conscious moved in mysterious ways!

We waited patiently for some time and I was about to move to another room when the miracle began to happen. A flickering blue light swirled around the room; strands like fibre optics filled the air then surrounded the bed... they were here then, the Blue Veins of the Clear Conscious! Slowly the bed linen began to rise, filled with the shape of a man! A head materialized on the pillow and I watched in amazement as his eyes slowly opened as if from a long sleep. The man sat up in the bed, he was wearing light blue pyjama's that blended perfectly with the colour of the room and it was obvious that he was confused and slightly wary of the people sitting waiting for him. He moved as if he was sleepwalking as he stood up from his deathbed. His family then surrounded him and hugged him but he I could see that he was still not sure who they were. Gently, they led him past me and out of the room to his new life. I knew that they would take him home and care for him; it was his Acceptance time.

I turned back towards the bed. The strands of bright blue light were still there and they had formed a swirling Portal... I knew that they were waiting for me. I found myself strangely calm as I walked toward the doorway with a brave heart... This was it then, it was now or never! I stepped through the Blue Portal and instantly I felt like I was moving at a tremendous speed... perhaps even the speed of light! Kaleidoscopic colours flashed past me with a glowing metallic sheen; it was as if I was on a roller coaster in Hyper Space...

WARP TEN SCOTTY...

IT CANNOT BE DONE JIM...
THE DILITHIUM CRYSTALS CAN'T TAKE IT!

SPACE. THE FINAL FRONTIER...

I was Captain Kirk...
Sitting proudly on the helm of the Enterprise.

WHERE ARE WE, MISTER CHEKOV?
I... I DON'T KNOW CAPTAIN
THIS SECTOR IS UNCHARTED... UNKNOWN!

I stood up... I heard a voice in the distance...

RICHARD...RICHARD... STAR TREK IS ON!

It was my mothers voice calling to me.
I was playing football in the street...

I'LL BE THERE IN A MINUTE MAM...

TAKE US HOME SULU.
RIGHT AWAY CAPTAIN...

I was home. My Washington home. I was in the back garden beside the rose bushes. There was an easel complete with canvas behind me with a small table full of oil paints and brushes beside it.

DO YOU NORMALLY PAINT FLOWERS RICHARD?

A voice but not my mothers...
A cold voice like a computer called HAL...

NO, NO OF COURSE NOT. WHY WOULD I?

***ROSES ARE SO BEAUTIFUL ARE THEY NOT?
THEY CUT YOU BUT THEY ONLY PROTECT THEMSELVES.***

THEY FLOWER AND DIE SO QUICKLY THOUGH…

***THAT IS SO TRUE… SO TRUE…
I BELIEVE IN SLOW DEATH, DON'T YOU?***

I stood in front of the blank canvas and looked to the roses.
White roses, pink roses, red roses…
I felt compelled to draw them, paint them.
I drew their shape in an outline…
I picked up a brush and began to paint them.
White, pink… BLOOD!
The red paint was not oil; it was blood…

***WHAT IS WRONG RICHARD?
WHY HAVE YOU STOPPED?***

I was shaking like the fragile leaves in the growing wind…
My hands began to tremble…

I DO NOT WANT TO PAINT FLOWERS…

BUT THE BLOOD RED IS SO APPROPRIATE IS IT NOT?

*NO… NO… I PAINT TO MUSIC
MUSIC I LIKE…*

AHH, LIKE THIS PAINTING…

I was no longer in the garden…
I was standing in my sitting room…
Looking directly at the The Bogus Man.
The last painting I ever did…
The Hi-Fi switched on and the music started…

> *THE BOGUS MAN IS ON HIS WAY*
> *AS FAST AS HE CAN RUN*
> *HE'S TIRED BUT HE'LL GET TO YOU*
> *AND SHOW YOU LOTS OF FUN…*

> **THIS PAINTING I LIKE RICHARD**
> **THIS MUSIC I LIKE…**
> **WHY DO YOU LIKE IT RICHARD?**

> *IT'S… BRYAN FERRY, ROXY MUSIC*
> *HE'S FROM WASHINGTON, SAME BIRTHDAY AS ME…*

I looked at the dark blue painting and was still proud of what I had achieved.
Subtle shades…
Subtle lines…
And the perfect Bogus Man,
Blood red at the side,
Skull face, creeping with menace…

> *I LIKE ACCIDENTS IN ART*
> *I DON'T LIKE ACCIDENTS IN LIFE…*

> **BUT IT WAS NO ACCIDENT RICHARD.**

> *NO ACCIDENT, WHAT DO YOU MEAN?*

> **COME WITH ME RICHARD…**

JOIN US AND YOU WILL UNDERSTAND.

My blue painting darkened…
Menacing shades of grey filled its landscape…
The bold lines turned to black wires…
Black snakes slithering with the Bogus Man towards Washington…
Towards my home…

THE BOGUS MAN WAS HERE… I COULD HEAR HIM!

ARE YOU SCARED RICHARD?
SCARED OF RESPONSIBILITY?

WHAT DO YOU MEAN?

YOU WRITE BOOKS NOW?

YES… IMAGINATIVE STORIES…
SUPERNATURAL STORIES…
WHITE PALMS…
BLOOD MIRACLE…

BLOODY MIRACLE! MORE LIKE, DON'T YOU THINK?

WHAT DO YOU MEAN?

…STORIES OF THE CLEAR CONSCIOUS
WHO WOULD BELIEVE THAT THESE DAYS?

THE CLEAR CONSCIOUS IS FINISHED!
WE ARE WINNING…
THERE IS NO 'TOWARDS HEAVEN!"

NO, YOU ARE WRONG
I WILL PROVE YOU ARE WRONG...

PUBLISH AND BE DAMNED, RICHARD?

I WILL NOT BE DAMNED AND NEITHER WILL MY SON!

VERY NOBLE RICHARD
BUT YOU ARE NO FIGHTER...

I ONLY LOST ONE BOUT...
AND THAT WAS BECAUSE I WAS DRUNK!
MY FATHER...WAS A BOXING CHAMPION IN THE ARMY
I COULD HAVE BEEN... A CONTENDER
I PLAYED FOOTBALL, THE PUNCHBAG WAS ONLY A WAY OF KEEPING FIT...

CONTROLLING YOUR ANGER RICHARD?

YES... RELEASING AGGRESSION, PUNCHING, HATING...KILLING!

YES, THAT IS BETTER RICHARD.
THE BLACK WIRE IS CONNECTING WITH YOU...
DON'T YOU FEEL IT?

Black snakes crawled and slithered from my painting...
Down the wall leaving slimy stains, across the floor beneath me...
To my feet, my legs...
They crept slowly up my body,
Curling tightly around me...

DO YOU LIKE SPORT RICHARD?

YES... I TOLD YOU.

***I LIKE SPORT RICHARD
THIS IS THE SPORT I LIKE
IT IS LIKE FISHING...***

A dry, hollow laughter filled the room.

***I'M A FISHER OF MEN RICHARD.
YOU COULD BE TOO...***

NO, NO, YOU BLASPHEME!
ARE YOU RELIGIOUS RICHARD?

NO... YES!

DO YOU PRAY?

YES... PROBABLY... EVERY LOTTERY NIGHT...

AND DID YOU WIN?

OF COURSE I DID NOT.

***YOU'VE WASTED TIME AND MONEY THEN?
HAVE YOU KNOWN HARDSHIP IN YOUR LIFETIME RICHARD?***

*YES, I SUPPOSE I HAVE...
MONEY ALWAYS SEEMED TO BE A PROBLEM.
IT SHOULD NOT HAVE BEEN.
IT WAS JUST THE WAY THINGS WORKED OUT FOR ME.*

THINGS COULD HAVE BEEN BETTER HAD YOU PRAYED TO US!
THINGS STILL COULD BE BETTER FOR YOU...
EVEN NOW.
THERE IS SO MUCH TO DO...
AND WE ARE WINNING!
THINK ABOUT IT...
THIS IS A GREAT RISK YOU TAKE RICHARD...
YOU ARE NOT AWARE OF WHAT IS AHEAD OF YOU.
CHANGE DIRECTION RICHARD.
THERE IS A FORK IN THE ROAD...

My room evaporated, my painting dissolved...
I was in the Hillsdown pub again, though it was not the Hillsdown I remembered...
Bryan Ferry's Olympia was on the Jukebox...
It was dark...
It was night...
And the stars were not blue; they were red...
Dying at the end of the universe...
And the night sky reflected that.

A full moon shone its ominous light into the pub...
Like a searchlight illuminating a prison.

The light was dim, creating threatening shadows...
Dark figures stood talking, drinking,
Sporadic laughter as...
The 'Creatures of the Night' looked at me.
Girls in skin tight clothes and mini skirts
With heavy black make-up, jewellery and tattoos.
Skinny Vampires in Fatfield...
Red eyes glaring...

Was I the victim in their horror movie?

Anna Calvi came on the Jukebox….

There was a smell of drugs and depravity…
This was not a nice pub anymore…
This was the outskirts of Hell!
The temperature rose suddenly…
I remembered heat…
I remembered thirst.

> ***WOULD YOU LIKE A DRINK RICHARD?***
> ***GO TO THE BAR…***
> ***THEY WILL NOT BITE YOU.***

I had been in rough pubs before…
It was a shame to see the place like this.
I would have a drink…
I would try and find out what I was doing there…

I moved tentatively to the bar.
The dark figures moved aside reluctantly to let me in…
Where a lonely Guinness waited for me…

> ***DRINK RICHARD.***
> ***RELAX AND ENJOY OUR HOSPITALITY.***

I took a sip of the ice cold drink.
The thick, rich liquid immediately refreshed me…

> *WHERE AM I?*

I said to no one in particular.

> ***THE HILLSDOWN PUBLIC HOUSE, RICHARD***
> ***DON'T YOU RECOGNISE IT?***

THIS IS NOT THE HILLSDOWN...
AND WHO ARE YOU?
WHY DO YOU NOT SHOW YOUR FACE?

I'M THE OTHER SIDE OF THE ARGUMENT RICHARD
THE KEY TO YOUR HIDDEN DESIRES...
PLEASURE BEFORE BUSINESS, SO TO SPEAK...

Then out of the shadows of the bar,
Walked Jeannette…
She was the one who had been speaking,
Only the voice had softened…

> ***It is good to see you again.***
> ***You said that you would be back.***
> ***Can I get you something stronger?***

NO THANKS JEANNETTE, NOT YET.

She looked different…
Taller, her breasts fuller, her lips redder… and her eyes…
They were hypnotic, intoxicating and delicious…
She was a Siren and I was instantly washed up on her rocks…

> *Song to the Siren…*
> *Did I dream you dreamed about me*
> *Where you hare when I was fox*
> *Now my foolish heart is leaning*
> *Broken lovelorn on your rocks*

> ***I hope that you are going to stay with us.***

We can be together forever...
Do not worry about the last world.
This world is all that matters.

Last world?
Lost world surely...
I was lost...
But I felt safe with Jeannette...
Someone who cared for me...

>   *YES JEANNETTE,*
>   *I WILL HAVE THAT DRINK NOW...*

Jeannette reached for the Bombay Sapphire,
And poured out two large glassfuls...
She placed the drink in front of me then reached over the bar...
And kissed me fully on the lips.
Her tongue was like an electric eel...
It seemed such a long time since I had kissed someone.
A latent feeling of love stirred inside of me...
Waking like a slumbering beast.

>   *I am puzzled as the new born child*
>   *I am riddled as the tide*
>   *Should I stand amid the breakers*
>   *Should I lie with death my bride...*

Wherever I was,
I would stay here with Jeannette forever...
I was lost in that bar...
Trapped by my own desires.

Anna Calvi came on the Jukebox again...
And everybody began to dance.

The sky is getting dark tonight
Darker than the fear that's gonna pull us apart...
I wanna lay in the dust
The dust is gonna fall here when I lie
God knows it's just the devil in me
The devil that's taking my hand to the fire...
It's just the door to the devil gathered in disguise
Taking me by the hand
And leading me, leading me off to the fire...

Jeannette began to move sexily in her tight black leather...
And enticed me to join her.
The never-ending party had started,
Welcome to the Pleasure Dome...

We drifted in slow physical ecstasy across the floor...
Then the sound of motorbikes,
Roaring menacingly outside...
Broke our bewitching spell.

The pub doors opened slowly...
And they walked in...
A blue light from the bikes headlamps shone brightly behind them.
They lit up the pub...
And the dark figures cowered, the blue light distasteful to their eyes.
Then everything changed to black and white!

I almost laughed out loud when I saw who was leading these bikers...
It was Marlon Brando...
And his gang from the fifties movie...
The Wild One.
Black leather jacket and blue jeans...

New York biker hat cocked to the side.
His gang members muscled their way to the bar
And the Vampire clientele were not happy,
The Bikers were in a mean mood...

Brando brushed past me and went to the Jukebox.
He slammed it sharply like the Fonz...
And the Black Rebel Motorcycle Club came on...
Guitars blasting through a tense atmosphere...

> *I wanna feel the light, I just can't receive*
> *Don't wanna leave the ground, I just need some air*
> *I need some air...*
> *It's not the prayer that you repeat at night*
> *It's not the Saint that has seen the light*
> *It's just the breath that you hold inside*
> *Just keep your cool it will be alright...*

Brando began to bop...
Then he turned to me...

> *COME ON MAN, WE'VE GOT TO SPLIT,*
> *IT'S TIME FOR YOU TO HIT THE ROAD...*

Jeannette's face changed....
A demonic look possessed it...
Her eyes turned red and her voice changed...
Deep and loud...

> ***YOU DARE TO INTERFERE***
> ***WHO DO YOU THINK YOU ARE?***

> *ME? ...I'M THE WILD ONE!*

Jeannette struck out at Brando...
And scratched his face,

Deep nail scars that bled thick blood.
His leather-gloved hand touched his wound...
Then he slapped Jeannette hard on the side of the face...
She fell to the floor...
Then all Hell broke loose...
The pub exploded in violence.
Bikers versus Vampires...
Screaming, terror, murder...
I was caught up in a surreal scene...
Threatening my sanity and I was scared!
A biker's switchblade slashed one of the dark figures...
He collapsed, covered in blood... dying!
I stood in disbelief...
Frozen monochrome.

HE HAD IT COMING KID
HE WAS PAST FORGIVENESS...
COME, WE GOTTA GO DADDY-O...

He grabbed my arm...
And dragged me to the door...
Jeannette still lay hurt on the floor.

NO... JEANNETTE!

THAT AINT YOUR GAL BUD!
SHE THE DEVIL IN DISGUISE!
COME...
WE HAVEN'T GOT MUCH TIME...
THE JOINT WILL BE FULL OF THEM SOON!

Brando whistled loudly...
Which was a signal for his gang to retreat.
He dragged me out of the pub to his bike...

GET ON, QUICKLY…
THERE IS A PORTAL OPENING!

The word Portal clicked in my mind.
I sat on the back of the powerful bike…
And we roared away at Hellcat speed…
His bloodied and beaten gang, following…

We were being chased…
A huge, heavy shadow followed,
Hot on our trail…
I did not dare look behind…
My imagination would not let me!

They closed in on us,
Hideous screams, getting louder…

Then a blue light flashed at the side of the road…
Ahead of us…

THIS IS IT KID, HOLD TIGHT…
I'M GONNA GET YOU THERE
EVEN IF I HAVE TO DIE TRYING!

The Black Snakes had reached us…
The living Dark Wire…
Reaching for our souls!
Brando revved his bike,
And we hurtled towards the light…

A tall tree…

Solid and unforgiving…

Time began to slowly move fast…

I remember now a tiny heartbeat…
Fluttering like a fragile bird.
I was curled up…
Safe from harm…
Floating in the fetal position.
Then first breathes…
Wheezing, coughing…
I spluttered out "where am I?"
My head was swimming…
Headache building, pounding…
Then electricity from my mind…
Coursing through my body upwards…
Crashing out of the top of my head!
Towards…

I was growing…
Breathing regular…
Heartbeat stronger…
Then lightning flashing all around me…
Was that the sound of thunder?

Its alive… alive!
…

PART TWO

Chapter Seven

THE BLACK WIRE

Waking gently, I swear I could hear the soothing sounds of Brian Eno hovering above me. Angelic music, ambient smells, clinical and antiseptic assailed my senses. My whole body ached with intense pain as I turned slowly onto my side; my head was sore and I was lying on a bed of crisp white linen.

My eyes flickered open and the blurry blue green colours of a hospital room greeted them. The light was too bright though, so I quickly shielded my eyes with my hands. Flashing multi-coloured diamonds shimmered on the peripheral of my vision and I was afraid that I was about to have a migraine attack... but that was the least of my worries. As I sat up on the side of the bed, I wondered where I was... and more importantly... who I was!

A young nurse came into the room and I could smell her perfume, rich and almost overpowering to me... why this seemed unusual was a complete mystery to me at the time. She was looking for something in one of the compartments at the side of the first bed...

"Nurse... Nurse..." I whimpered but she did not seem to hear me and promptly left the room. I stood up weakly and felt very fragile on my feet; I stumbled to the end of the bed and held on firmly as I was sure that I might faint. I was fully clothed and wearing a black leather jacket and I noticed that my hands and face were sweating profusely. I thought that maybe I should sit back down on the bed and gather my thoughts but something was motivating me... muddled messages in the back of my mind were telling me that there was something that I had to do.

I walked out of the room into a busy corridor. Doctors and nurses passed by me, busy people in a busy job. I called to them but they ignored me, it was obvious that I was not a priority case. The heat of the hospital suddenly increased and an immediate raging thirst came over me; I knew that I had the symptoms of some sort of a fever so I went to the nearest Men's room for water. Inside, I turned the tap on at the first basin. Cool water caressed my hands and soothed me, it seemed so refreshing... it was if I had never felt water before. With such an absurd thought in my mind I bathed my face and as I did I looked up into the wall mirror...

Nothing!
No face...
No me...
?
An anxious laugh passed my lips...
But this was not funny...
My mind began to panic...
My heart thumped loudly...
My throat felt dry and barren...
I looked again into the deceitful mirror but still no reflection greeted me. I shut my eyes and I think I began to pray...
Please Lord... please...
I opened my eyes again...
And still nothing...
I wanted to shout out but no sound came...
I'm dreaming... I must be!
I hoped...

I stepped back from the mirror...
The reflective surface now revolted me...
It was cheating me, taunting me...

Then someone entered the room from the door behind me...
He went to one of the basins to wash his hands...
There was blood on his fingers!
I stood still, silent, my breath heavy and fretful...
"Are you alright? You do not look too well..."

He could see me! It was not a dream!
I looked back into the mirror...
But there was still no reflection!
I began to feel anxious again... I felt faint.
"Perhaps I can help you, I work here..."
His voice was dull and familiar but this thought was not an immediate concern...
"I will get you something to drink, something to calm you. Do not go away..."
For some reason I did not trust this small man, I knew that he must have worked at the hospital but there was something about him that unnerved me. Shortly after he left the room I too decided to leave... Perhaps I was having some sort of psychotic episode? Whatever was happening to me, I felt paranoid and claustrophobic. I knew that the hospital was probably the best place for me but I wanted to get out in the fresh air and cool down. I looked for the main entrance and made my way there... I was not aware that I was being followed.

Once outside the building, a refreshing cold breeze blew through me and instantly calmed me down. It was quite sunny and the light irritated my vision, I instinctively reached into an inside pocket and found a pair of blue tinted sunglasses for my sensitive eyes.

I went and sat down on a visitor's bench opposite the main doors. I felt like I needed a cigarette even though I knew that I did not smoke. I bent over and held my head in my hands. What I had just experienced was impossible... surely!

My mind had just blocked out my face...

That is all...

My face? ...What did I look like! I somehow remembered that I'd had amnesia before but that was a long time ago...

So what was this then? ...Acute depression? ...Drink? Or was it some sort of negative reaction to some drug?

Had I been in an accident? ...My body still ached so this was feasible. I looked at my leather jacket but there were no cuts and no damage; then the thought hit me, why did I still have my jacket on? Surely it would have been removed in any emergency. Suddenly there was a searing sharp pain in my back... I thought that perhaps I should return to the hospital; maybe that would be the best thing to do.

I looked to the hospital main doors and noticed that the man who had gone to get a drink for me was standing there, casually smoking a cigarette. He was looking directly at me but it was not a concerned look... there was something about him that made me feel cautious. Something that I did not want to remember...

The enigmatic man stood there staring at me for some time and I thought that I could see a wry smile on his face as he looked at me. Feeling fearful of him I stood up and walked away. Perhaps it was the fact that I was feeling alone and vulnerable or perhaps it was just simple paranoia... whatever it was, I knew I that I had to move away from him.

I walked past the hospital car park onto the main road; a nameplate on the small library opposite indicated that it was Kayll Road. Looking at the old library triggered memories... memories of a small child...

I was upstairs at the front of a bus...
Looking out at the tops of passing buildings.
Chimneys smoking in the distance...
An imaginary monkey was following alongside...
Jumping and swinging from roof to roof...
Looking like a simian Spiderman.
If I lapsed my concentration, he would fall behind...
The bus stopped at the crossroads...
Just to the right of where I was standing...
A bingo hall and Steels Social Club were nearby....
I watched as the young boy walked towards the library and entered.
Inside a world of books awaited...
A world of imagination...
I went to the Mythology section...
Tales of Brave Ulysses...
Mighty Thor and Ragnarok.
I left the library a happy young soul.
Books in hand, I sped home.

Home did not materialize to me though; I still could not recall my name. Clouds of despair formed over me and I felt depressed as I looked towards the library. A strange sensation warned me that I was still being watched and this did not help ease my dilemma. Perhaps my coat would reveal who I was, I checked my pockets contents... a bunch of keys, car keys that included a door key with a Vaux bottle opener and the robot from Futurama. There was a brown wallet in my jacket and I quickly opened it hoping that it would reveal something. There was money inside, quite a lot I was surprised to find and an anonymous library card but there were no bank or credit cards, no driving license, no names and no numbers but there were faces.

A black and white picture of a young nurse, a picture of two young boys... I looked to the children, I knew that they were probably my sons but no memory of them came back to me. The young nurse was surely my mother... I tried hard to recall her name... Bessie, Betty came to mind... Elizabeth! But there was no surname. It was a glimmer of hope though, something to work on...

I remembered that she lived somewhere in Ryhope village...

"This church is always here..."

Suddenly echoed in my mind... and a vision of Ryhope Church and the Reverend Wilson appeared. This was a starting point then... but how to get there? I walked down Kayll Road to Chester Road; I had money to pay the bus fare into town.

At the bus shelter, a young man and a woman waited. They seemed to be arguing about money... rent money, drinking money... money for fags. The woman was watching over a toddler in a pushchair and she seemed to mostly ignore the young man's vitriolic words. I noticed that there were no wedding rings. I thought at one point that he was going to slap her with the back of his hand... perhaps I should intervene, say something to this annoying man, then I thought better of it. I noticed that they did not seem to be aware of me so I decided to keep quiet as I had my own troubles to contend with.

A bus heading to Sunderland came along and I knew that I would be able to get a bus to Ryhope from there... the sooner the better I was beginning to think! As the young girl struggled onto the bus without any help from her partner, I opened my wallet and took out five pounds...

"Sunderland please..." I said but there was no reaction from the driver, he simply started the bus and drove on. A sinking feeling began to rise in the pit of my stomach as I sat down slowly in one of the front seats... I decided that I would try and ignore this feeling of not existing, for that is indeed what it was beginning to feel like! I was not some ghost floating aimlessly about; I was real, I was solid! I could feel the cold, the wind on my face; the sweat on my brow... I could not fly or walk through walls; that would be just too absurd to contemplate. It was just that there were some rude, ignorant people in this world; that was all.

All my hopes were pinned on this Reverend Wilson then, perhaps he could help me, perhaps he knew who I was and what had happened to me... a myriad of questions began to swirl around my mind and in no time at all the bus reached the station in Sunderland.

I stood in the Park Lane bus station and looked for the Ryhope stand. The bus terminal was not how I vaguely remembered it... I found myself in a brand new gleaming station and not the old simple design I was expecting. I found the stand I needed and a bus was already there, waiting to leave. The door was open and the driver was sitting patiently, reading a newspaper...

"Ryhope please..."

The driver did not look at me; as he seemed to be too engrossed in his paper, probably page three or the sports pages I assumed. I went upstairs and took a seat at the front. As soon as I sat down the engine started and the bus pulled slowly away from the stand.

I remembered that I used to enjoy bus rides as a child; you could sit back, relax... and think. Perhaps I had suffered some sort of a stroke or possibly a mental breakdown but what was I doing in Sunderland General? I somehow recalled that Cherry Knowles would have been a more likely hospital in those circumstances. These were anxious thoughts as I looked out at the passing scenery that was now growing more and more familiar. The large breaking waves of the North Sea calmed me and as I sat in a dreamlike state, the journey became a blur... but I still had that paranoid feeling that I was being followed.

And I was...

A small black car with dark, tinted windows was following slowly behind.

As the bus approached the sharp bend at the bottom of Ryhope Village, I knew where I was. We passed the War Memorial monument on the village green and I knew that the next bus stop was mine. I pressed the red bell and went downstairs. The bus stopped just before a bend in the road and as the doors hissed slowly open, I passed the driver who seemed to be completely baffled as to who had rang the bell. I had no time to dwell on this though as once I was off the bus, instinct compelled me to look behind it. There was not a lot of traffic on the road, only a black Chrysler car; one of those that could quite easily grace the set of any Batman movie, was parking slowly beside the village green. I watched it stop... but nobody got out.

I crossed the road at the zebra crossing; I knew that the church was literally just around the corner to the right. In less than five minutes I was there. I stood at the walled entrance and looked past two tall trees towards the church. I had a strange feeling that I had been there very recently... only the sky was a faultless blue on a summer's day.... I looked to the sky above the church, it was sunny but a cold winter wind blew across it. I sensed that there was a storm approaching... the weather was definitely about to change.

The wind seemed to whisper to me as I walked up the pathway to the church door...

Tell him I forgive him...
Tell him I forgive him...

These words swirled in my ears as I entered the open church. Inside it seemed empty, there was nobody about. A ghostly silence filled the hall evoking a peacefulness that instantly soothed me and made me feel safe. I went and sat at a front pew and prayed. I clasped my hands hard together and asked God for his help. My eyes were closed while I prayed but as I slowly opened them, I was aware of a faint blue glow around my hands... it was as if there were two strands of light coming from them! I kept my hands tightly together and as I continued to look at them, my hands seemed to shimmer and blend into the floor; they appeared to fade away and disappear in front of me... then I could see them again! It was like some special effect from the science fiction film, Predator and I laughed at this quite loudly as I knew that my mind was still playing tricks on me. This was not the response to my prayers I was wanting.

Then a voice to the left of me broke my disappointing thoughts...

"Hello there, I hope I have not disturbed your prayers..."

It was the vicar of the church. A young, stout looking man with a slightly receding hairline and a kind face was standing to the left of me. He smiled as I stood up to greet him....

"You... you can see me?" I stuttered naively. I knew that this question had instantly sent alarm bells to the vicar but he hid his reservations well as he replied...

"Well, I know my sight is not what it used to be but I think I can just about make you out!"

I was relieved by his light, humorous reply and it made me smile. I felt instantly at ease with this man and my trust in him was immediate.

"I'm sorry... it's just that I... I have not been too

well…"

The vicar fell silent and thoughtful for a moment, he knew that I was a worried man. Then he asked me to sit with him, to talk with him and he would do his best to help. He asked me what my name was…

"I… don't know," I said and then I told him about awaking at the hospital. Then I had to ask him…

"Are you Reverend Wilson?"

"No, my name is Robinson, Paul Robinson. I do not know of any Reverend Wilson I'm afraid. Is that why you came to Ryhope church?"

"Yes… that is part of it…"

I reached for my wallet and then showed him my mother's photograph…

"This, I am sure is my mother. I think her name is Elizabeth… but I do not remember her surname. Do you know her?"

"I'm afraid I do not. I think that maybe this picture was taken a little before my time."

Again, his comments brought a smile to me but also disappointment, as I was still no further forward in my quest for enlightenment. The vicar stood quiet for a moment and looked towards the Altar; I knew that he was thinking about what he could do to help me.

Then he turned to face me…

"Perhaps you should not have left the hospital. I do have an idea though… have you heard of Cherry Knowles?"

Yes I knew of Cherry Knowles, I knew that it was another hospital and for some reason the name sent a shiver down my spine… then the face of William Shields suddenly appeared in my mind. I could not remember this man's name at the time; to me it was just another piece of a very frustrating jigsaw. As I pondered this intrusive vision, Reverend Robinson continued…

"At Cherry Knowles there is a Geriatric ward... maybe there will be someone there who will recognize your mother?"

At once I knew that this was a good idea and I agreed to go there without hesitation, I was so grateful for the young vicar's help.

"Come then, we'll take my car, the hospital is not far from here."

Outside of the church, I noticed that the sky had darkened dramatically as we walked to the Reverend's car. I looked out towards the sea where a heavy grey mist indicated that rain clouds were making their unwanted way inland. We got into the Reverend's silver Renault and then set off for Cherry Knowles.

As we prepared to turn right onto the Stockton Road, I was drawn to a row of houses opposite the junction, houses I vaguely recognized. Again my mind was flooded with the memories of a small child...

Toy soldiers, cowboys and Indians...
Hi Ho Silver away!
Cricket in the garden...
Firing catapults...
Throwing boomerangs into the air...
An older girl who I knew to be my sister, smiling at David and me...
Magical walks underneath a low train tunnel to the beach...
Starfish and whelks...
Crabs and seaweed...
Small fish trapped in shallow pools.
This was not my home though...
I was with my cousin who was the same age as me...
Suddenly a heavy sadness filled me and I yearned to be back there...
Happy days, carefree days...

The warm days of my youth...

Then my melancholy was broken, the car had stopped and we were in the visitor's car park.

"Here we are... you had me worried there. You were so quiet."

"I was... remembering."

"Good... good. Anything significant?"

"Not really, just memories of bygone days..."

I had been daydreaming and what I should have done was stop the car and go to that row of houses as they may have triggered more memories but I was at the hospital now and my priority was to hopefully find out who my mother was...

We entered the hospital and the Reverend went straight to the nurse on reception as I waited a few paces behind. It was obvious the nurse knew the Reverend as the pair chatted for some time. At one point the nurse glanced quizzically at me then continued to talk to the Reverend. Eventually he indicated that we had been given the green light to proceed and after we had received our essential visitors badges we made our way to the Geriatric ward. The hospital was busy... nurses and porters were quietly going about their important business with purpose and dedication. For some reason though this scenario seemed wrong to me. The hospital in my mind should have been empty and silent. I knew that this did not make any sense and it puzzled me.

We walked on further into the hospital and as we passed one door in particular, I stopped suddenly. Reverend Robinson seemed concerned...

"Are... you okay? What is it?"

My hand reached slowly to the door and gently touched it...

That man's face again...
William Shields...
Warning me...
Another Reverend...
The Reverend Wilson...
Then a feeling of pure evil...
Walking towards the door...
Behind the door, hissing...
Breathing heavy, sinister, snake like!
I called out " Be gone vile creature!"
But it was the Reverend's voice not mine...
Then I felt warm hands on my shoulder,
Comforting me...
It was the Reverend Robinson...

"Hey... hey, it's okay... you are safe. I am here with you."

I wiped my clouded eyes and his caring kind face was looking at me...

"I'm sorry... something was..."

"Don't worry, something like that was bound to happen sooner or later. Memories are coming back to you. You have to be prepared for those that are not welcome!"

The Reverend was right, there was a rocky road ahead of me but it was a path I had to take. We continued on to the Geriatric ward where a nurse who had been notified that we were on our way greeted us

She took us into a private room and introduced us to a frail, elderly lady then left us. The woman was called Jill and was presumably of a similar age to my mother...

"Hello Reverend, it is good of you to visit again. I find it so hard to get to church these days."

The Reverend knew the woman from his regular ward visits and went and held her hand...

"Don't worry Jill, you know that God is with you here in your room…"

The Reverend then went on to explain why we were there…

"The reason for my visit Jill is this good fellow. He hopes that you may be able to help him. He has… had some sort of an accident and has lost his memory. He has a picture though, of a lady who may be his mother and if you could recognize her then this will help him greatly."

"Oh I will try Reverend, I will do my best although my sight is not what it used to be you know. Come here son, sit on my bed and show me the picture of your mother…"

I went to the bed at sat down gently beside the kind woman. I opened my wallet and showed her my picture. She placed her thick glasses on and reached into a side drawer for a large magnifying glass…

"Ah… of course I know this woman. It's Bessie… Bessie Pirum!"

I could feel tears welling in my eyes as the old lady looked at the photo of my mother… at last I knew her name!

"Bessie lived on Brick Row in the Aged Miners bungalows. Her brother Dick lived just up from the green there. Tragic, tragic… he was killed in the Bahamas, knocked down while saving his grandson…"

Joan went quiet for a moment and I did have a memory of this, a newspaper cutting that proclaimed my uncle a hero…

"Bessie was a lovely lady, well liked in the village. She is buried in the cemetery with the rest of her family."

I asked Jill if she knew what Bessie's children were called but she could not remember and I could tell that already this visit was getting too strenuous for her. I hugged Jill and thanked her, as I knew that we were tiring her. I don't think that she was used to many visitors and this was sad. The Reverend whispered a little prayer to her then we left the room.

"Well, we now have a name for you to work on... I am sure things can only get better from here on. Now, there is someone else I have to see."

The Reverend went to the Doctor's room opposite and entered without knocking... I sensed that something was wrong. I waited patiently for a short while then it suddenly hit me... of course; he is trying to get me committed! He wants me to stay here until I am well. I knew that he only had my best interests at heart but I felt that I could not be locked away... I still had a strong feeling that there was something urgent I had to do and to be able to do it meant I had to be free.

I decided to leave and leave fast. I looked at the passing nurses and orderly's and felt that I was being watched. I walked quickly down the corridor towards the entrance, I did not run as I thought that would arouse suspicion and I thought I heard the Reverend calling for me as I approached the main doors but I did not look back.

Once outside I did run, as fast as I could down the long hospital road to the main road where I turned left to head back towards the village. I was surprised by how fit I felt considering the aches and pains of the morning. It was now snowing lightly outside as I turned left into Smith Street... I was instinctively heading towards the cemetery. I stopped at William Terrace and turned left, the cemetery was only yards away and the snow was already beginning to cover the ground...

RYHOPE CEMETERY

As I entered the cemetery I knew that the layout was familiar to me. Straight ahead was an old, derelict and foreboding building that seemed to be a forlorn remnant of a bygone age. Ancient, tall gravestones loomed over me as I walked to the place where my mother lay. The Reverend had been right, now that I knew her full name; doors were being opened to me... I knew exactly where her grave was and went straight to it without delay.

A young tree marked her final resting place, which I found heart-warming as it's thin branches seemed to comfort and guard the ground where she laid at peace. I stood before it and wept as the words on her gravestone crushed my heart instantly...

    PRECIOUS MEMORIES
    ELIZABETH PIRUM
    WILL LOVE YOU ALWAYS

I could hear prayers being said...
Softly falling like the snow...
Then shadows formed around me...
A cold wind in my face but no snow...
Only a bright blue sky...
Above another day...
My mother's coffin was being lowered...
Into the dark, dark ground.
Faces appeared to me...
Faces I recognized.
Faces that were welcome...
Some that were not!
I fell down to my knees and grabbed the ice-cold grass in my hands...

I must have been kneeling like that for some time as the light snow had begun to lie on my shoulders. I stood up and stepped back, I wiped my eyes and then noticed the gravestone behind my mother's. It was a white cross and for some reason I was drawn to it. The light snow that was falling around it shimmered on the simple gravestone as I walked with some trepidation towards it... I rubbed the snow-covered cross and read the inscription... it cut through me like some deep, dark dagger from my subconscious...

Lay down easy, stars in my eyes...

I knew these words...
I had requested them!
They were words from a song...
I knew the name of the person buried there...
IT WAS MY NAME!

Cold, cold reality... not some sick joke...
A stinging realization that froze my mortal body...
Hands shaking with ice cold fear...
The shadow of the Reaper was laughing in the snow...
My heavy heart began to beat like it would burst at any moment.
I staggered back and fell...
My hand cut on the sharp soil...
Blood!
How could that be?
Hysterical laughter, in my head began to take control...
The edge of madness and mayhem beckoned...
Swirling images on fast forward...
My mind was in turmoil and in grief.
This was not paranoia though... this was real!

I looked to the white cross and I knew that I was dead!
My memory was returning but I did not want to face it...

Perhaps it was only a nightmare…
I hoped and prayed that I was still in Cherry Knowles under some sort of sedation…
Dreaming some sort of weird dream!
But the cold snow dispersed such wishes…
I was sat in front of my own grave…
I remembered buying it!
£264. 85...
I used to joke… probably the only land I will ever own!

My voice trembled as I slowly began to sing…

> *Lay down easy, stars in my eyes*
> *Try not telling too many lies…*

This was no lie though… this was the warped truth!
That had hit me like a rocket…
A reality that I did not want to accept…
ACCEPTANCE… that was important….

I continued to sing the song at a heartbroken pace and continued to feel sorry for myself although I knew that self-pity was dangerous…

> *Wake up feeling not foolish or wise*
> *And life goes with me no matter what size…*

Then I felt a presence singing with me…

> *Laugh till I'm tired, sing till I'm dry*
> *'Cause life is a moment you pass with a sigh*
> *Never comes back sure as yesterday's by….*

Standing before me…
Wearing sunglasses in the falling snow…
With a drab, grey raincoat from another era.

Memories of that coat...
Began to fight to the surface of my mind...
"I know that song, a seventies hit is it not?"
This was a question I could answer...
"Family... my favourite band..."

My memory was returning as I visualized a manic Roger Chapman belting out the vocals! Things were getting surreal then but I still had to be cautious... who was this man?

"Ah I see that you do not recognize me, the coat, the sunglasses... white snow irritates my eyes. I am the man from the hospital who tried to help you this morning!"

I stood up quickly; I did not want this man to see my name on the gravestone. If I was dead then surely there were rules... nobody must know what I am....

It did begin to make sense then... the nurses, the bus drivers, the people who cold not see me. My hands in the church... I was controlling the disappearance act; like the Invisible Girl from the Fantastic Four...

But how did he see me when there was no reflection in the mirror?

My instincts told me to be wary of this man as the stranger in the grey raincoat continued...

"I've been following you, I was worried that you might need help."

"I... I'm okay now. It was seeing my mother's grave... it upset me."

"Look Richard, my car is just over there," he pointed to the black Chrysler at the bottom of the cemetery...

"Why don't I take you home..."

It was strange to hear my name being said but how did he know it?

"Home?"

I thought of the picture of the two boys in my wallet. I knew now that they were my sons, Robert and JJ... I began to tremble as more memories retuned but I concealed my feelings from the man as best I could. I had to keep myself together as I was being bombarded again by thousands of sudden thoughts.

"Yes, that would be so kind of you... this weather is getting worse!"

Chapter Eight

WASHINGTON

The snow was falling much heavier as I warily got into the black Chrysler. Everything seemed to glow pure white but the clouds were breaking in the distance... a glimmer of blue in the winter gloom. The man in the raincoat removed his sunglasses to reveal eyes that were cold and dull...

"Where to then Richard... where is the place you call home?"

"Washington..." I said with conviction, I knew now that my house was on a road called Bridge End.

We left Ryhope Cemetery and turned left towards Burdon Lane. This narrow country road would take us to Shiney Row, then onto Washington. The man drove as carefully as he could as the snowfall was hampering his vision. I turned to him and realized that I knew this man from somewhere, even the dated unfashionable raincoat was somehow familiar... my memory circuits whirred into action but unfortunately there was no definite recognition. I felt a little uncomfortable sitting next to someone I did not know...

"I was wondering how you know my name..."

He was silent for a moment then replied...

"Oh... I checked the hospital records..."

This reply seemed unlikely. If I had died then he would know this... he would not be sitting calmly beside me, giving me a lift home! I knew that thoughts like this would undermine my sanity... I had to keep my head together, not just for my sake but also for the sake of my two sons. I was still walking the Earth for a reason and they were it!

I needed to know what this man was called, this

would help me to recall who he was…

"You have not mentioned your name my Good Samaritan…"

The man continued to look straight ahead as he concentrated on the dangerous snow covered road…

"My name is… Eamonn… Eamonn Hunter. I guess you would call me an Agency worker, y'know hospital porter, casual worker…"

"I thought you were a Doctor?"

"No, no, nothing so grandiose… too much hard work and not enough reward!"

I thought this a strange statement…

"And you, what do you do Richard?"

"I wa… am a Supply Teacher. Art and P.E."

"Ah nice subjects, simple and creative. I suppose you find teaching very fulfilling do you not?"

"I don't know about fulfilling, I do know that it is bloody hard work doing Supply…"

Memories of 'hard' challenging classes came back to me… at least that was in the past now, I thought with humorous relief.

We crossed the Houghton dual carriageway and were now driving towards Shiney Row… I knew it would not take too long to get to Washington. This Eamonn Hunter was still an enigma though… why was he being so helpful? If he was an Agency worker then surely this was beyond his call of duty… to follow a man he was worried about and then take him home. It did not add up so I was on my guard… but perhaps I was being too paranoid. There were nice people in the world and perhaps he was just one of them!

We approached the Washington Highway and Eamonn had been quiet, I broke the uncomfortable silence…

"I would like to thank you Eamonn for the lift home in this weather…"

No problem Richard, I know Washington quite well... I used to live here myself some time ago..."

I did not press him on this because we had reached the Galleries turn off.

"If you could just turn left here I will get out... my house is not too far."

Eamonn reluctantly stopped the car beside a large circular shaped church...

"Are you sure I cannot take you to the door?"

The offer was quite appealing considering the cold weather but I still did not trust him, there was something about him... a memory deep inside of me that was not ready to surface...

"No, this is fine Eamonn... thanks once again" I said, then quickly got out of the car. The snow had stopped falling and the grey clouds had moved on but it was now early evening and dark...

"No trouble at all Richard... I look forward to seeing you again!"

As Eamonn pulled slowly away in his black Chrysler, I knew that this was a strange thing for him to say... when would he see me again and why?

Now I had to be careful, I could not risk anybody recognizing me. I thought that I should not be seen... and then I began to fade away.

I watched in amazement as my hands, my arms and my legs shimmered unnaturally in the crisp winter light... although I could see myself; I knew that others could not see me. The realization that I could do such a thing caused a sickness in my stomach... it was unnerving to say the least but it was something I was going to have to get used to, something I was going to have to do for the sake of the people that knew me!

I stood for a moment and looked at my hands, the effect was exactly as I had witnessed in Ryhope church.

It was as if I was the creature from Predator I thought or maybe it was more like Star Trek and a Klingon cloaking device was shielding me. Whatever the effect it was obviously the most unusual feeling I had ever known... and yet it seemed so natural. I was invisible to the world of man and as a ghost that made much more sense to me; I was thankful for that thought as 'things making sense' was exactly what I needed right now!

I had started walking and had been lost in deep thought when I suddenly realized I had reached my road... I knew exactly where I was and where my house was and continued on towards the end of the road. A woman in a heavy coat walked past me like I did not exist... wasn't Klingon technology marvellous! I joked to myself. A minute or so later I was there... 55 Bridge End.

As I stood before my old house in the spooky shadows of a tall tree, I braced myself for heartache... I did not know how I would react to the sight of my sons; it felt like an age since I had seen them. The branches of the bare tree seemed to grip me and hold me fast as I stood staring at the dark house...

There were no house lights on and no sign of life. What day was it? I suddenly realized that I did not know. JJ's distinctive white Mini with the red stripes of the England flag covering it; was not on the drive so it was safe to assume that he was not at home. I walked to the front door and reached for my keys. I checked around quickly before I opened the door but most people were inside keeping warm, I suddenly felt like a furtive burglar about to sneak into my own home!

I opened the door quietly and turned the light on, if Robert and JJ did turn up then they would simply assume that one of them had left it on. I walked past the kitchen to the front room... all was as it had been; it was as if I had not left. It should have felt like ages since I had stood there in that room but it did not, in fact it felt the opposite. I felt warm and safe and that was touching... but there was also a tangible sadness in the air.

I looked to the silver carriage clock, with a picture of my mother holding baby Robert. It was seven thirty so I set my SAFC wristwatch and then I pulled the garden door blind up to the beauty of a picturesque winter scene. It was a strange feeling knowing that I had missed Christmas. The garden also brought back sad images of my dog Arnie, playing carefree in the snow. I somehow knew that his free spirit was alive and was safe somewhere and that comforted me. I then decided to look upstairs for clues as to where my two sons were. First I looked in Robert's room and it was surprise to find that it was tidy... One thing was missing though, his laptop. Wherever he was, he was probably going to be staying there for some time.

I then went to JJ's room and was shocked at the state it was in... JJ had never been renowned for being the most tidy of people but I had never seen his room like this before. Clothes were strewn across the floor, amongst dirty plates, glasses and a mass of neglected CD's. Empty cans and bottles of Vodka and Whiskey littered the place; food and drink stains covered the carpet... I sat down on his unmade bed and surveyed the carnage... even by JJ's standards this was not normal. Something was desperately wrong... then the date on my gravestone appeared in my mind and I realized...

26th SEPTEMBER 1955 to 26th SEPTEMBER 2010

...It had been some time but he was still grieving!

I felt so sorry for him, sad that he had obviously loved me so much. I wanted to find him, tell him that I was alive, sort of...

"Look JJ, I'm dead but I still exist!"

What a revelation that would have been, that all the pain and worry of life finally had its reward! But I knew I could not... the risk to his sanity would be too great.

So where was he then? If his room were in this state, then what state would he be in? I became worried like any normal parent would be, surely if he was drinking heavily then he would not be driving. Okay, his dad was dead but that was no reason to become so desperate. Robert had carved out a good life for himself as a session musician, working and gigging around Sunderland and Newcastle. He was also building something of a reputation in London and I always assumed that one day he would probably move permanently south to follow his dream in full. JJ was currently studying for a Degree in music at the Sage in Gateshead and was in a band called Chasing Jayne. He had already cut a demo album of his own songs so maybe success for him was just around the corner too. I always felt that one day they would probably form a band together as they were incredibly gifted musicians.

I left his room and resisted the urge to tidy it... what sort of burglar would break into your room and clean it? I laughed at this refreshing thought and pondered what a better world it would be if things like that actually happened.

Before I went downstairs I looked into my room... again, all was as it was before but there was a different feeling to it now... it was as if it was a shrine. I could not touch anything... I dared not... perhaps I would be trapped here forever! I shut the door quickly and went to the kitchen.

I felt like I wanted a cup of tea or more importantly a beer! ...I was sure that I was thirsty though and was that normal for the dead? As I looked at the kettle, I noticed a notepaper next to it. The tidy handwriting was instantly recognizable as that of Roberts...

> *JJ,*
> *I'm stopping at Matt's this weekend,*
> *Got a gig in Edinburgh.*
> *Turn your phone on and I'll phone you*
> *Try not to drink so much*
> *It will not bring Dad back!*
> *Rob.*

My hand trembled as I read his note... perhaps he was wrong though; perhaps his drinking had brought me back? Maybe that was why I was here, to somehow save my son! JJ was still upset about my death but what I could do to help? Robert had always been the more emotional of the two whereas James had always been more like his mother, so in some respects this response of his was the most surprising.

My anxiety about JJ's state of mind increased... I questioned myself again, is that why I was here? Something in the back of my mind was haunting me though... almost teasing me. I had to find him...

"I know, I'll phone his mobile... no you bloody idiot, you cannot do that!" I countered immediately then I realized where he probably was... the nearest pub!

THE OXCLOSE INN

I left the house at once; the pub was literally only a five-minute walk away and was next to JJ's old secondary school. The snow was now quite deep but it felt a lot warmer than earlier. Teenagers were throwing snowballs at each other on the small field beside the pub and young couples were waiting in the bus stop opposite, dressed up for a night on the town. I guessed that it was probably Saturday.

When I reached the Oxclose Inn I walked in unnoticed... the Invisible Man was in the building. First I looked for JJ in the main lounge, which was quite full but there was no sign of him. I then went to the small bar room opposite... and there he was, slumped on the end of the bar like the proverbial barfly. It was only eight thirty and he was loaded. JJ had the look of a rock musician that was definitely out of it as he sat there dressed in his black, hooded leather jacket. His hair was longer than I remembered and the slight beard he always used to have was more prominent. As I looked at him my heart went instantly out to him... I wanted to go straight to him, talk to him but I knew that I could not. It was obvious that JJ had been drinking for hours and I sensed that the barman was beginning to lose his patience... my paternal instinct kicked in and I knew that I had to get him home.

I went to the empty toilets and materialized. For the first time, I realized that controlling the effect was proving to be quite easy but what I had to do next was not. JJ was simply blind drunk, there was no way he would recognize me and to make doubly sure I would deepen and alter my voice. Before I left the Gents, I glanced in the mirror and it was not a fifty five year old looking back, it was a young man with thick brown hair cut in that fifties Ferry style that I used to like. JJ would definitely not recognize me; in fact I had to feel my face myself to check what I was seeing!

"C'mon JJ, you've had enough lad... I'll order a taxi for you."

Jimmy the barman was in the process of turfing JJ out...

"Uh... no... I'll... another pi... pint Jim..."

"I don't think so son, you've had enough! Time to…"

I strolled behind JJ and interrupted Jimmy…

"I'll take him home Jimmy, I've... just got here but I can see he's wrecked…"

Jimmy looked at me cautiously…

"And who are you then mate? I don't recall seeing you in here before."

I knew I had to turn the accent on to help convince Jimmy…

"Why aye man, me an' JJ are good marra's… went to school together…"

"Schoolmates eh? And what school was that then?"

"Oxclose… what's this Jimmy, do you not believe me man? I know Dan and Bobby too, they're JJ's best friends, I thought they might be with him."

"They were but they've gone onto a party somewhere and JJ was just not up to it as you can see but like I said son… I don't recall seeing you in here before."

"I've been in here a few times man but I haven't seen JJ for awhile and I heard that he was going through a rough time."

"Aye, rough time alright and that's an understatement considering what he has been through… poor soul. He's been saying strange things lately…"

"Aye, that's bound to happen when you hit the bottle…"

"Hit the bottle? …If only that had been all he'd hit!"

Jimmy's last words puzzled me but I did not have time to contemplate what he had said, JJ seemed to be attempting to listen to this conversation through his drunken stupor and I knew that he was probably close to passing out so I had to move fast…

"Ha… way man Jim… jus one more…" he

mumbled weakly and there was a hint of violence in his voice.

"You better get him home son... you know where he lives then?"

Jimmy was still checking me out...

"Of course, I told you we're marra's."

"Shall I order you a taxi?" said Jimmy...

"No, I'll try and walk him home... the fresh air might do him good."

"Well don't say I didn't offer..."

I put my arm around JJ and helped ease him from his barstool.

"Haway JJ, time to get you home big man."

The people sitting drinking in the bar were mostly men who shook their heads with disdain as we stumbled past them to the door...

"Hey... where're we going... and who the fu... are you?"

We were outside and JJ was swaying from side to side on the slippery snow, this was not going to be easy..."

"I'm... I'm an old friend JJ... and I'm going to make sure that you get home safe and sound."

JJ lifted his head and looked at me in the clear winter light but I knew that he could not see me; my face must have been a drunken haze.

"Tha... that's good of... you. I think I've had a bi... bit too..."

"Yes JJ, you've had a bit too much. Now shut up and concentrate on putting one foot in front of the other, this bank is a bit too steep when you are full of beer!"

We must have looked like a couple of stereotypical drunks as we staggered up Raby Road. Luckily there was nobody about when we reached home, no inquisitive neighbours with prying eyes.

"Give me your keys JJ and I'll open the door."

I had to be careful about what he might remember, although I knew that the chances of him remembering an 'old friend' who helped him home were rather slim.

Once inside, JJ managed to negotiate the stairs himself and the last words I heard him mumble were...

"Cheers... mate... we'll have a drink... tomorro..."

I heard him slump heavily onto his sturdy metal bed and that was that... mission accomplished!

I went downstairs to the kitchen and opened the small fridge that I'd bought mainly for cool beers and was pleased to find that it was full of Guinness. Robert was away, JJ was as drunk as a newt; it was time for me to try to relax and unwind... it had been one hell of a day!

I went with a six-pack and sat in the front room, greedily drinking the cold Guinness as if there was no tomorrow. I knew that there were probably still bottles of Gin in my room if I needed them but the black stuff was like nectar and it was all I wanted. It seemed like months since I had enjoyed a refreshing pint so I simply slumped back on the sofa and drank... I did not switch the telly on or my cd player, I sat in silence and thought about the day... the day I found out that I was dead!

It really was too much to take in and I could not shake the feeling that I had been through this before for some reason. My head hurt as I considered where I was and why I was! ...I thought about the kindness of Reverend Robinson and felt sorry that I had ran away from him but I was glad that I was home now, safe and sound. Then I thought about the man from the hospital that had given me a lift home and pondered why I did not trust him... his old fashioned raincoat repulsed me for some reason but I couldn't work out why.

I finished the last beer and realized I felt drunk... and very, very tired. If I was a ghost then, how come I was so exhausted? How come I could taste things, feel pain and bleed? ...I looked at my cut hand but it was not serious, just a scratch. Questions like this were swirling around my head like a maelstrom... and I was just a humble spirit with no answers. Perhaps this was it then, this was the afterlife... death was not the end, just the continuation of watching over those you have loved. My eyes became as heavy as my heart; it was time that I slept too so I made my way up to my old bed...

Sleep was instant and so were the dreams...
A young girl in a flowery dress, skipping...
Carefree in a wood...

Ring a ring a roses
A pocketful of posies
A tishoo, a tishoo
We all fall down...

I was home again...
But there was no Robert, no JJ...
No snow...
The dark sky was blue...
Blue stars that shone without a moon...
Then... a blue sky appeared that held no sun.
I knew that this was my world now...
Acceptance.
Then sonic e-mails in my sleep...

Help me Lord, please...
I did not mean to do it...
There was somebody else...
Something else inside...

These words woke me…
Sweating and scared…
Fear filled the house…
Like a dark cloud…
Thick and sickly…
These were not my words…
It was JJ talking in his sleep…
But I had heard them before…
They had called to me…
Brought me here…
Was I dreaming? Was this real?
I slept again…
And this time there were no more dreams.

Another bright morning broke into my room; I could tell that it was not snowing, at least not yet. I sat up and thought about JJ, about what he had said during the night…

I did not mean to do it…
There was somebody else…
Something else inside…
…and who was the little girl in the rose patterned dress?

I stood up and went to JJ's bedroom, he was still heavily asleep and by the look of it he was going to be like that for some time. The poor lad was going to have one hell of a hangover that was for sure. I went back to my room and dressed… clean jeans and another thick, warm blue shirt. I then went downstairs for breakfast.

Tea and toast, then everything was washed up and put away. I did not have to worry about things such as bread and beer being missing; as I was sure JJ would not notice this when he awoke. Even if he did he would probably assume it was the mysterious friend who had helped him home. I checked my watch, it was 10.00 am and I had overslept. When I was alive I would have had my usual bacon and eggs on Sunday, then I probably would have gone for a run with Arnie. I felt slightly guilty that I had risen so late.

So what was I to do now, sit around and wait for JJ to wake up? And what could I do then... ask him what his nightmare was? Why was he praying for help? I paced around the house... I was frustrated, I was helpless ...I did not know what to do and I felt like praying myself! I needed some air, I had to get out of the house and think. It was Sunday and perhaps I needed the comfort of old friends...

Chapter Nine

THE COMRADES

It was surprisingly warm for a February morning and from the kitchen window I could see that the snow was already beginning to thaw slightly. I had decided to go to Seaburn to see how my business venture with my friend Steve Nanson had turned out, as I never did get to go to the opening party. From there I would visit the Comrades Club in South Hylton because that was where two other friends, Kevin Rafferty and Dickie Lincoln were likely to be. So I had a full day ahead and the prospect of possibly being able to see Steve, Kevin and Dickie again really excited me, as it now seemed an eternity since I had spoken to any of them.

The reason I wanted to see them was not just the comfort of familiar faces; it was also the fact that I might find out about what had happened to me and more importantly, what had happened to my son JJ. My dilemma though, was that if they saw me they would probably recognize me, especially Kevin who had the best memory of anyone I had ever known. I went to the hallway mirror and looked at my youthful self. I concentrated as hard as I could to try and change my facial features but nothing happened, I guess things like that only happened in the comics or the movies and unfortunately I was not Mystique from the X-Men. I stood still for a moment, something else was bothering me... how was I to get there? Then I realized that my car should still be in the garage and I had the keys. I stepped outside and cautiously opened the garage door... but my car was not there! I quickly closed the door and went back into the house. The fact that my car was missing puzzled me but I concluded that maybe my eldest son Robert had borrowed it for some reason, maybe his car had broken down or was in the garage for a service or something... the big mystery though was where was JJ's car? More questions then... and that I could do without. I ordered a taxi.

The taxi was prompt as usual but I could tell that the driver was probably a bit hung over from Saturday night, as small talk during the journey was limited. I didn't mind that though as I knew that idle chat might lead to probing questions and that was something I did not want.

We drove down the A1231 towards the A19, then over the motorway and onto Sunderland. At the Wessington Pub roundabout I looked up Ferryboat Lane and a strange tingling passed through me... I knew that I had relations nearby, my aunt Mary lived in Castletown. She was the last living member of my father's immediate family and I was tempted to visit her but of course I knew that I could not.

We sped on past the turning to the school where I used to work as an Art teacher and fond memories instantly returned. The pupils that attended the school were similar to the pupils of Pennywell, where I had also taught; both schools had their fair share of down-to-earth rough diamonds that could be hard work if you did not know how to handle them. My philosophy to teaching had been simple 'what you give out, you get back' and this had been my mantra throughout. And what a football team I had managed at that nearby school; full of young eager players, some of which had the potential to make it as professionals if they were given the chance. The North East had always been like that though, a hotbed of soccer talent... where most of the time young players slipped through the net, I began to think of my own school friends and myself... but I had been daydreaming; we passed the Stadium of Light then turned left at the Wheatsheaf to head to the seafront. Within minutes we had pulled in front of the Fried Black Stuff and what a sight for sore eyes it was, the crisp winter sun was gleaming brightly on its large neon sign and it really was something for me to behold.

I stepped out of the taxi and generously paid the driver, I noticed that Seaburn was more or less deserted; a few people were walking with their dogs along the promenade opposite and one or two hardy runners were braving the harsh winter sea breeze blowing in briskly from the North Sea. I drew in deep breaths of salt air then turned to have a good look at what I had traveled from Washington to see.

The Fried Black Stuff Blues Diner had been my brainchild... when I had been alive in that despondent flat in Oxclose, JJ and Robert used to come and stay at weekends. I only had four hobs to cook on, so frying was always the order of the day. Inevitably that meant music and beer while I was cooking... and of course I would always drink a little too much, which would result in meals that were, how can I put it ...a little overdone!

"Fried black stuff again lads, I'm afraid..." I would regularly say and the name for my particular type of cuisine eventually stuck.

Then one day Steve Nanson phoned me from Edinburgh out of the blue and announced that he was retiring from Advertising and that he was going to return home and put money into something but he did not know what...

"Fried Black Stuff..." I exclaimed...

"Fried what?"

"A blues diner... y'know, like the ones they have in America. We'll make a fortune man..."

"We?"

"Well it is my idea Steve..."

"Aye, sounds great Rich. Let's do it!"

Steve and I had been friends since we had attended Sunderland Art College together as young, naive art students. I remember well, our very first lesson on a bright September Monday morning... it was a life drawing class and while we prepared our paper and pencils, the model walked boldly in and proceeded to strip fully naked and then pose seductively on the studio bed. I remember turning to Steve who was set up at the easel next to me and we both had large grins on our young faces that were as wide as the Wear. I think I said something like...

"Aye, I think I'll definitely be back here tomorrow then..." which promptly cracked Steve up and we have remained friends ever since.

So here I was, standing in front of a dream that two old friends had made come true. Of course the interior had not been finalized when I was alive so I couldn't wait to see inside. I walked to the large windows and peered in. The wide blinds were open, which indicated I assumed that the early morning cleaners had been active. The diner was closed though and I was not sure if it would be opened during the winter days... or maybe it would open around twelve like the pubs and clubs.

My ice-cold breath kept clouding the windowpane, which I constantly had to keep wiping but it was worth it. Inside, the finished article was just how I had envisioned it... Steve had kept his eye on the ball and had done a thorough job. Our diner had not been based on those fifties motorway diners, we had decided to go for a thirties city feel... and we had done it! I was as proud as any dead man could be.

Time was moving on though and there was still no sign of Steve. I guessed that Big Jo, the cook we had hired might be preparing stuff in the kitchen but I had seen enough. We had achieved what we had set out to do and we had done it in spades!

So it was now time to make tracks to go and see old comrades. I thought that I could probably get a taxi at the Roker hotel so I set off along the seafront for a bracing walk along the cliff pathway. The sea air was so refreshing as I made my way towards Roker and as I looked out to sea, memories began to flood back to me...

Football on the beach...

Dodging crashing waves on the Cat and Dog steps...

When I was young we used to visit Seaburn regularly.

Sometimes we cycled there...

Sometimes we went by bus...

But it was always a canny day out.

We knew that we were lucky to live beside the sea.

Reliving the past helped pass the time and it was not long before I was at the hotel, inside a taxi and on my way to South Hylton. It had been a nice morning and a journey worth taking so far but as I sat in the taxi an uneasy feeling returned... I was again convinced that I was being watched and followed!

I tried to put this to the back of my mind as on the journey over to Pennywell and south Hylton, I had plenty of time to think about my lifelong good friends. Dickie had been plumber all of his life and Kevin or Raff as he was more commonly known, was a shipwright. They were both fully paid up clubmen and Sunday lunchtime drinking was sacrosanct to them. I had gone through school with both men; enjoyed football, music and beer with them and now I realized that I had not spent enough time with them in my later years. But life could be like that; eventually you slowly drift off on your own... a lonely path that ultimately has only one destination. The closer we got to the Club the tenser I became. Not being seen by them was paramount; the thought that I would suddenly pitch from the dead and go for a pint in the Comrades was just too surreal and inconceivable. So obviously I would have to go in there incognito.

It did not take long to get to the Comrades; I paid the cab driver and then disappeared. This was going to be difficult and I knew it. To see old friends that I had known for fifty years and to be not able to talk to them would surely test my mettle. I swallowed hard then entered the club.

I walked past the doormen unhindered and went silently to the bar. I had to be careful not to brush anybody, I could not be seen but I was still solid. The length of the bar was relatively short considering the size of the room that included a large snooker room extension. I stood at the right end of the bar and surveyed the Club... and there sitting in front of me were Dickie and Raff. They were sitting facing a large screen on the far wall, their backs towards me... but it was them alright, resplendent in the red and white stripes of Sunderland AFC.

I looked to the screen and realized that our team was about to play Fulham, a Sunday match that was being televised. The pre-match build up was being broadcast and I took this turn of events as a very welcome unintentional bonus. It was a small table that my two friends sat at and they were near enough for me to hear what they were saying. As I looked at Dickie and Raff the passage of years just slipped away, of course both were slightly grey in the hair department now and Dickie sported the shaved head look that I had preferred but as they sat there enjoying their drinks it was as if we were all seventeen again. The three amigos back together... of course the fourth amigo; our old friend Mick Averre was still in South Africa where he had emigrated to some years ago.

Raff's laugh was as infectious as ever and I longed to sit beside them and join in with their banter. How long I could stand and observe them was uncertain as a strange mixture of a happy sadness overcame me. Raff was the slightly taller of the two but Dickie was more robust being a veteran weightlifter. Both of them were well built though and strong from years of hard physical work... they were men not to be messed with and I was proud of them.

Dickie then stood up and took his place at the busy bar; I noted again his striking resemblance to the actor Chris North from the American crime series, Law and Order and remembered that I had always forgot to point that out to him. I shuffled further back into the corner of the bar and had to sidestep people as I moved; I was sure that some of them seemed to sense my presence but the lively atmosphere of the bar soon dismissed any potential awareness.

The kick off for the match was scheduled for three o'clock and already the bar was in full swing. The Comrades was a typical North Eastern working-mans club that was prosperous and popular, a shining example of what a good club should be. Its main clientele were solid, working class people who were mainly from the Pennywell and South Hylton area; people who worked hard and played hard. I had never seen any trouble in the club on any of my visits but like any pub anywhere, arguments could happen.

I listened hard to what my friends were saying but there was no mention of me; that is until the football match started. Raff looked sad as he turned to Dickie and said...

"Aye, Richie would have enjoyed this one, he has a

friend in London who supports Fulham. I can see him now sitting beside us..."

Dickie looked back at him quite sternly...

"Raff man, you know what we agreed..."

"Aye alright Dickie, I'll not mention him again..."

Both fell silent for a moment then in unison they both picked up their pints and drank a toast to me...

"Cheers Richie old son ...wherever you are!"

He's behind you said the phantom pantomime in the back of my head...

These words were like a piercing arrow to the heart and a tear formed in my eye, I was so glad that I was invisible... Big boys don't cry in Pennywell.

I suddenly needed a drink and was aware of the sharp smell of gin on the bar beside me. The man who had bought the gin had taken a round of pints to his friends and was coming back for the chasers. I drank one of the gins so swiftly that nobody saw the glass move then discreetly placed money on the bar for the drink. The look on the man's face when he returned was comical. He picked up the empty glass and looked furtively around, then had a go at the barman about the missing gin. The barman was equally perplexed at the extra money that had appeared from nowhere.

I suppose I could have had free drinks all afternoon this way but my mother had raised an honest boy and anyway I wanted to keep a clear head in case I missed anything. I stood patiently and listened carefully but Raff and Dickie were true to their word, nothing more was mentioned about me. I felt tired now, emotionally and physically and was having thoughts about leaving the club when the match started... Sunderland versus Fulham in the Premier League. I decided to stay... Haway the Lads!

Unfortunately the match proved to be disappointing and resulted in a frustrating goalless draw. A muted air pervaded the club but Dickie and Raff looked set for the night and ordered more drinks. It was time for me to go though but before I left my secluded spot, I noticed somebody that I vaguely seemed to recognize... a young man was standing at the opposite side of the bar and was arguing with the man in front of him. This young man was obviously drunk and in a mean mood. I looked at the man and tried to remember from where I knew him. I knew that he was bigger now, thicker set with a big head that was not in proportion to the rest of his body. He had wild, staring eyes and a wide mouth that held large protruding teeth but it was not just his appearance that revolted me it was his whole demeanour...

He started to get angrier and the more vicious he became, the more familiar he became to me. I did know this man... I had taught him Physical Education at Pennywell Comprehensive when he was younger. He had been an evil, malicious bully when he was at school and it was obvious that things had not changed that much. A sickly feeling filled my stomach as I looked at him...

Then I saw the black wire, writhing from his legs to the floor... they moved and squirmed like they were part of him and I knew that I was the only one who could see them. In the back of my mind I had seen these black tentacles before but my memory of them was hazy, like a nightmare you did not want to recall. As I watched these living wires, they became more active and like a nest of snakes they crept slowly up his body. His appearance became darker and more sinister; a green mist surrounded him and hissed from his mouth as he breathed... the mood of the Comrades suddenly changed and everybody seemed to freeze like living statues. It reminded me of a TV advert I had seen where the man pretends to be at work when his wife phones but he is really having a drink with his friends in his local bar; this made me smile but this situation was not funny.

The angry mans appearance now reminded me of Doctor Jeykll's altar ego, the evil Mister Hyde... but that had been me had it not, only somewhere else... the feeling of something wicked trying to claim my soul made me feel sick. This was a hazy nightmarish memory I did not want to recall... I began to shake and I felt weak; the sense of malevolence in the club was so tangible I could hardly breathe. I knew that something foul was about to happen... then the young Mister Hyde suddenly went quiet. Without warning he struck out at the man he had been threatening. The man went sprawling into the back of Raff and Dickie and knocked their drinks onto the floor. In the confusion at the bar I noticed him reaching for a knife in his left trouser pocket... I instinctively intervened and grabbed his hand...

"Do you want some too?" he spluttered violently into my face.

He could see me... I was visible! I could only hope that in the resulting melee my appearance had been shrouded but before I had time to worry about this he struck me hard with his right hand. I fell back against the bar and banged the back of my head and as I lay crumpled and beaten on the floor... I noticed that the angry man had dropped his knife.

Dickie and Raff sprang at him with two other big men who bundled the school bully out of the club without hesitation. I think I heard the doormen giving the troublemaker a taste of his own medicine as I struggled to remain conscious. Like I said earlier, they did not mess around here...

My friends came back into the bar, which had settled down quickly like some saloon from an old

Western, the broken glass had been immediately cleared and it was as if nothing out of the ordinary had happened. Dickie and Raff came towards me and I was still stunned; I did not have time to exit or disappear... I held my bloodied face with my left hand in a feeble attempt to partially conceal my features. Dickie picked up the knife and placed it on the bar, while Raff looked at me and spoke...

"That was great mate, you stopped somebody getting stabbed there..."

He stopped speaking suddenly and I knew what he was thinking...

"Jesus... you look like..."

I knew that Dickie was staring at me too...

"Who are you?"

"I'm... Jason" I stuttered, "You probably knew my uncle... he used to drink here with his friends..."

"You're Richie's nephew?"

"...Yes, I've... just moved near here and thought I'd watch the match in my new local. It's not always like this is it?"

I was thinking on my feet and they had bought it... I had remembered to alter my voice, which added to the bold deception. I had been lucky that I had been standing directly behind my old pupil when I materialized, lucky that the barman was elsewhere... because like I have already mentioned, it was simply too much for anyone to accept that I would simply return from the dead to watch a football match in the Comrades!

Raff was still inquisitive though...

"I don't remember seeing you at the funeral..."

"Oh, I was there alright," which was not exactly a lie, "I think I wore shades most of the time, it was a sad day..."

"Aye you're right son, a sad day for all of us... but

hell man, you're the spitting image of him when he was younger," Raff exclaimed.

"Yes, I've been told that I look more like my uncle than my dad."

"Well Jason..." said Dickie, "You've done your family proud; you may well have just saved someone's life. Come and have a drink with us."

I looked around for the potential victim but he had gone, probably did not want to get into trouble with the Club and I wished I could leave too but the damage had been done... and anyway I simply could not resist having a drink with my old friends, it was an offer I could not refuse.

Before I sat down I quickly removed my coat and placed it on the back of the chair, I was well aware that Raff or Dickie might recognize it although I was not sure if they had seen it before. This was going to be tricky but I decided I would not stay with them for long and as I sat chatting with my friends, I concentrated hard on every word I said. It was difficult pretending to be my nephew but it was worth it... when would I ever see them again? Perhaps I could come back again as Jason I thought hopefully but the risk was too great. I had got away with it this time... next time I might not be so lucky, one word one slip and then God knows what might happen. It was not fair to put my friends in such a perilous position.

I had tried to find out what had happened to me but Dickie and Raff would not talk about it... we basically only talked about football and for a short time for me, things seemed normal...

But things were not normal... what were those black wires that I had seen on the angry man? Surely there were not natural, or were they? And that feeling of pure evil that surrounded him… had it forced me to materialize? It was as if it had sensed my presence. These thoughts scared me and then I thought about JJ… it was time to get back to him.

Chapter Ten

BRIDGE END

Pennywell taxis were close to the Comrades and within half an hour I was back in Washington. The snow had more or less thawed but it was still winter and still bitterly cold, the brisk February wind that swirled around my house in Bridge End was sharp and unforgiving. My home seemed dark and lifeless in the quiet night and loomed before me like a giant stranger. I did not bother to go inside, as I knew where JJ would probably be. I made my way to the Oxclose Inn.

I was slightly drunk and this helped ease the pain in the side of my head where I had been struck. I tried again to remember the name of my assailant but I could not… it was definitely him though. The voice was older but the vicious venom that had come out of his mouth was the same. I suppose I was surprised that he was not already in Prison, although it was obvious that it would not be long before that was where he would reside. Just the thought of him made me shiver. I remembered how I had to stop him from hitting another pupil when he was in year ten and I remembered that in all of my years of teaching, he was probably the most malicious pupil I had ever come across… a pupil that longed to hit the teacher. In fact, I think he was excluded at one point for staff assault.

Well he had hit me eventually but I had stopped him knifing someone and for that I guess he owed me somewhat. You can get through to most unruly pupils, work out what their problem is and help solve it. That is if you can be bothered… but with pure evil you do not stand much of a chance. For that was what he truly was… surely that sick black wire that I had seen attached to his body was feeding and controlling him. I knew that he was not alone... how many more were under the direct influence of this Hellish black wire?

This depressing thought stayed with me until I arrived at the pub, the night seemed much more colder now and the constant wind had picked up. There was definitely something in the air; I had an uncomfortable feeling that something was about to happen, a feeling that was becoming all too familiar... I entered the bar and JJ was there. It was Groundhog Day and he was unsurprisingly drunk again. Jimmy was wiping the bar top when he turned towards me...

"Well that's what I call timing... your marra is drunk again. Time to get him home I think..."

"Aye Jimmy, that's why I'm here. Come on JJ, your chauffeur is here..."

"Chauf..." JJ mumbled. He was in the same state as the previous night that's for sure and it was not a pretty sight.

"Yes chauffeur, except I've got no car. We gonna have to hoof it again."

"Who the hel... are you..."

"The same mate who got you home last night. Come on JJ, put your arm on my shoulder."

We struggled again up the steep bank against a fierce wind that was ferocious and unrelenting. Trees were lashing against each in the park opposite with an anger that seemed unnatural. It was a start of a windstorm that was obviously going to get a whole lot worse. Thankfully we did not get blown away though and eventually made it safely to our house in Bridge End. Once inside I helped JJ up the stairs and onto his bed, he did not seem as heavy as he used to be but I knew that he been neglecting meals for the comfort of the bottle. I felt so sorry for my son and also so helpless...

"Why are you doing it JJ, why are you drinking yourself to death!"

He suddenly became more focused but was staring out through his window at the turbulent night sky. He even seemed more coherent...

"Death... what do you know of death? I have seen death... sat beside him... but nobody believes me..."

This statement threw me completely and I was worried that he was sobering up but he continued to look straight ahead and not at me... he was remembering something...

"What do you mean JJ... sat beside him?" I had to ask. There was a moment's silence and I thought I could see tears in his sad eyes...

"...In the car. The crash... it was not my fault..."

"What crash JJ?" I asked but I could tell that he was getting angry...

"Nobody believes me... he appeared from nowhere... said he was there to end my life and make my family suffer... he pushed the pedal with his foot... but I managed to open the door and jump out... *it was not my fault!*"

JJ was too agitated now, I could see him shaking but I had to ask him...

"What was not your fault son?"

"I thought you were supposed to be a friend..."

His head was in his hands now, tears flowing freely from his eyes...

"I killed him... my car crashed into him..." he sobbed, "I killed my own father! But it was not me... it was... Death!"

JJ began to cry intensely like he was a little boy again and I... I staggered back in shock... If a spirit was what I was, then surely I was now as white as a ghost!

I stepped back slowly out the room onto the landing

and held onto the wooden staircase. A sickness in my stomach gripped me as hard as a vice, I went to the bathroom and tried to vomit but nothing came out. My son had killed me…that was why both our cars were missing. My own son was responsible for my death! This was too much for me… my head began to spin and I felt like I was going to black out. The walls of my precious home began to close in on me… I became too traumatized and I began to have an anxiety attack. A heavy cloud darkened my mind, my vision became blurry and my thoughts muddled. I could not come to terms with what JJ had said… he would not have meant do such a thing, I knew that but this was little comfort. I had to get out of the house… Who knows what a mad ghost might say or do…

I walked back towards the pub but I craved solitude so turned right towards the park. Nobody would be about at this time of night… I could sit and think and try to regain my lost sanity.

DEVILS WOOD - MIDNIGHT

I reached the large stone opposite Devils Wood and sat on the wooden bench next to it and let my tears flow freely. For someone who had not cried that much in his lifetime, I was certainly making up for it now.

To stop me having some sort of a breakdown, I had to think about what had transpired… JJ did not drink and drive and he certainly did not do drugs, whatever he saw would not have been imagined. He was a truthful person who was now a tortured soul in turmoil. I wanted to go back to the house and forgive him but I knew that would be fateful.

JJ had said that he had seen Death; it had appeared before him. An unseen passenger had entered his car then… surely this was a spirit like me, only one that was evil!

But why had I come back?
What could I do?
How could I answer JJ's prayers?
Time stood still in my mind until I looked at my watch... midnight!

I still had no answers, only questions, as I looked towards Devils Wood... a place where dark shadows moved with the swaying trees...

Then the wind dropped dramatically...
And the weather warmed.
Had I fallen asleep?
I had certainly drank enough...
A blue moon rose over Devils Wood...
And dripped its light over the trees...
Trees that were now fully leaved...
It was not winter anymore...
It was summer.
A warm breeze caressed my face...

NOBODY KNOWS, NOBODY SEES... I FEEL THE BREEZE...

A song in my head...
It soothed me in the still night...
But there were still shadows moving in the wood...
As the breeze whispered to me...

Tell him I forgive him...

I had heard this voice before...
A young girl calling to me...
A memory of disturbed dreams...

JJ had not killed her...
That was not why I had returned...
What did this girl want of me?

I walked toward the wood...
The trees threatening...
I stood on the edge not wanting to enter...

Tell him I forgive him...

Echoed through the trees...
The voice was now nearer, clearer...
I stepped into the wood...
Perhaps I was home in my Heaven?
And the nightmare was only beginning.

I walked into the wood, past the quiet trees...
Trees that were trying to warn me...
A warm wind covered my back as the wood became thicker...
Deeper I went until I reached the centre...
A clearing with a tall, solid oak tree...

And there she lay... in the darkness...
Alone and quiet...
The moon fought to shed its light on her...
But I could see her...
The young girl called Rose...
Motionless, dead!
From where I was I could see that her throat had been cut...
Savagely, without mercy...
And standing in front of me, directly above her...
In the grey raincoat that was too hot for a summers night was...
Eamonn Hunter...

Staring with no emotion at the dead girl…

I could not forgive him!
The rage inside of me was too great.
I was a volcano about to erupt…
The revelations of this dark night…
Were too much for me…
I was about to snap…
I could not control myself…

You evil, evil bastard!

I shouted…
He turned and looked at me…
But there was no malice in his eyes…
Only a blank stare I could not understand…

I ran at him as fast as I could…
Into him…
And through him…

I hit the oak tree at great speed…
Then…
Darkness.

THE GHOST OF DEVILS WOOD

There were no more dreams; I had dreamt enough… there was only the uncomfortable feeling of a wet wooden stick poking my hand! It was morning and a red light filled the sky…

"He's not dead man, look he felt that…"

I opened my eyes and was greeted by a sore head that thumped its pain into my bloodshot eyes… in the red haze I saw two young faces looking down at me…

"Get a picture… he may be a wanted criminal or

something..."

One of the schoolboys pointed his mobile phone at me and I panicked. I held my dirty right hand to the side of my face then disappeared in front of them! I stood up invisible and ran away... out of the wood to? It did not matter... anywhere...

I ran to the Washington bus station and sat down on one of the sheltered benches... I was out of breath and very confused as I tried to remember what had happened. I gradually realized that I had knocked myself unconscious when I had hit the tree, my head was not only bruised now but it was cut from the hard oak... red blood that could not be seen, dripped silently to the cold floor.

I was hurt and lonely. I had no one to turn to... or maybe I did. A Northern bus bound for Ryhope pulled up opposite me, perhaps I could talk to Reverend Robinson. If anybody in this cruel world could help me then surely it was he. I felt I had failed then; failed JJ, failed Rose... Evil spirits walked this Earth that were too strong for me, too cunning. I was bruised and beaten. I wanted to go home, my new home through the Portal. First though, I would ask Reverend Robinson to help JJ. Perhaps he would go and see him, talk to him. It was the best I could do. I knew that this would jeopardize my identity but surely a man of the Church believed in the Afterlife. This would be my gift to him... positive proof.

Chapter Eleven

REVEREND ROBINSON

"I thought you might turn up again Richard, you had me worried…"

The vicar turned to face me as he finished praying at the Altar. I was lucky to catch him at work early. He came towards me slowly then held my hand…

"You should not have run off like that, I was only trying to help you! Come and sit with me… you look bruised and battered. That is a nasty cut you have there, what in the world has happened to you?"

"I ran into a… bit of bad luck."

We sat at the front pews like we had when I had first met him and I immediately felt at ease but there was something different about him… something I could not define. He did not seem his approachable gregarious self but perhaps that was only because he was worried about me… or perhaps it was the shattered state I was in, I must admit I wasn't at my best perceptively. Maybe he simply had a dose of the Monday morning blues like most people, he was only human after all.

"Can I get you something to drink Richard? You look like you have been sleeping rough, not advisable in these weather conditions."

"No thanks Reverend, I'm not sure my stomach could take anything at the moment."

"Oh that is a bad sign…" he replied but something else was puzzling me…

"How do you know my name Reverend? You did not know it when I last saw you."

He stood up and seemed slightly flustered, as if he was stalling for time…

"I'll get you some water… and some paracetamol,

something to calm you. I can see that you are tired... Once I knew your mother's name, it was quite easy to source your name..."

He went to the Vestry and returned with a glass of water and two large pills...

"Here take these Richard, they will relax you."

I sipped at the water but only pretended to swallow the tablets... a mild paranoia had possessed me and suddenly I felt uncomfortable in the vicar's presence. He sat back down beside me...

"Tell me Richard, why have you come to see me?"

"I... I wanted to ask a favour of you. I hope that I am not being too presumptuous... especially after I ran away from you at Cherry Knowles."

Reverend Robinson seemed curious and I noted that he seemed concerned although his face did not hold the same kind countenance of a few days ago...

"Go on..."

"I... I must... no, I want to return somewhere as soon as I can... but I need your help!"

"Of course Richard, what can I do for you?"

"My son JJ; is in desperate dire straits mentally. I think he needs spiritual help, the kind of help that only somebody like you could give. I would like you to simply talk to him and listen to what he has to say... tell him that you believe him and that he is not wrong."

"Of course Richard, that should be no problem. It will be good to see him again..."

This last sentence slipped past me as he continued...

"Come with me to the Altar and we will say a prayer for JJ."

"Yes Reverend I would appreciate that... then I must leave, I must return. I am so grateful to you."

We stood and walked slowly to the Altar. I made the sign of the Cross over my chest but was still not sure if only Catholics were supposed to do that. We both knelt before the Altar and I expected Reverend Robinson to speak but he was silent. My hands were held tight together as I began to say a humble prayer for JJ... the blue strands I had seen before appeared and stretched from my fingers up to the roof and beyond but I carefully looked to the Reverend, I noticed that there were no similar blue veins coming from the his hands! I continued to look at him from the corner of my eye and for a moment I thought that I could see a smile on the side of his mouth...

It will be good to see him again... echoed in my mind and this time the sentence registered. I became instantly cautious... then my heart began to beat faster as I heard the Reverend try to suppress a muffled snigger. He looked sideways at me...

"What is it Richard, what is wrong? Did you take the tablets I gave you?"

I stood up gingerly as I felt unsteady on my feet; my head was spinning... I took the tablets from my jacket pocket and threw them onto the church floor...

"No... I didn't!"

There was a broad smile on his face now but it was not warm, not his...

"I think you may be having another anxiety attack Richard... perhaps I should call a doctor? I think we should get you back to Sunderland Hospital."

"Sunderland Hospital... that is where you really work isn't it!"

I looked at him intensely and my mouth trembled as I looked into his red eyes... It was not Reverend Robinson; it was Eamonn Hunter!

"I know who you are, you cannot deceive me anymore!"

The mouth of Reverend Robinson formed a large vile smile; that immediately mocked me. He was trying to suppress laughter...

"Well it was fun while it lasted wasn't it... so what are you going to do now Richard? You couldn't save yourself, you can't save your son... how in the world are you going to save the dear Reverend?"

"I... don't know... what I do know though is that we can die again here, really die... be gone forever!"

"Are these violent threats of revenge Richard?"

"Revenge?"

"Yes revenge, and just how do you aim to do that? Anything you do to me will hurt the Reverend... and anything I do to you will hurt you. It's just not cricket, is it old boy?"

I stepped back away from him and was wary of any movement by him, but there was none... There was a moment's silence that could have been an eternity in that lonely church...

"How about I give you a chance Richard, a chance for me to explain things to you. I would enjoy that... so why don't you come on in, the water's fine!"

What did he mean? I was momentarily puzzled as he stood there smiling insanely at me. Come on in? ...then I realized what he meant. He had possessed Reverend Robinson and he was hinting that I do the same. This was too unbelievable... this was a concept that belonged to church folklore but I knew now that it was true. I had to try and do what he had done and join him, I did not know how but I had to try. He was teasing me but I needed answers, some sort of closure... this was why I had come back!

"Come to me Richard, join with us as there is so much I want to share with you."

I walked towards Reverend Robinson; I knew that I somehow had to enter his body... and his mind!

The possessed Reverend's face began to change; a low rumbling of laughter began to seep from his twisted mouth... a laughter that resounded ominously around the cold church walls. Then a manic wide smile stretched across his face... he was no longer the amicable young vicar I had come to know and like, he now looked more like the demented Joker from the Batman comics.

His vile laughter increased but he did not move, he just simply raised his arms and then outstretched them in some damned mockery of Christ on the Cross...

"Come Richard, I am waiting for you..."

His eyes began to bulge insanely and his face turned a deathly white...

"Come to me... I am a fisher of men!"

This blasphemy maddened me and as I drew nearer to him I clasped my hands over my mouth and nose, as the smell of the Reverends breath was not to my liking.

Standing directly in front of him, it was as if the Reverends body had frozen solid but his mocking laughter still rang around the old church. He stood as still as a statue, looking like he was some evil parody of Christ and I did not know what to do. I nervously began to pray...

"Please Lord... help me. Show me what I must do..."

The Reverends laughter increased... the unpleasant smell that was emanating from some Hellish bowel increased. It seemed like I was trapped in some sort of time loop as I stood before the taunting joker. His mad laughter did not seem to be resounding around the church anymore... it was now firmly embedded in my mind...

"Please Lord... what am I to do!" I repeated... then suddenly a brilliant blue glow illuminated the church. Shimmering strands of light descended slowly from the ceiling above us and attached themselves to me. I felt their presence immediately flow through me; filling my veins with a renewed vigor and my soul with pure belief. Like a puppet, the blue veins moved me closer to the Reverend. I thought I could hear a Heavenly choir singing loud and glorious all around me but I knew that it was probably only my imagination. The blue strands lifted my hands till they touched the vicar's hands...

Cold and hard as ice...
I was trembling...
I gripped his hands as hard as I could...
I could feel blood...
Cold blood...
Dripping from my fingers...
The laughter in my mind began to hurt. It felt as though I was hanging on for my life...
Then I felt an energy inside of me...
Crackling in the pit of my stomach....
Surging electricity moving upwards...
One goal...
And from my mind it exploded into the Reverends face...
Blue light... blue heat...
I was merging with him!
One body...
One cross...
One...

CLOSURE

There was darkness in the Reverend's body and a smell that was musty and old. I moved slowly forward through a thick green mist, taking one tentative step at a time... It was like walking in a dream that was teetering on the edge of a nightmare. I began to sweat as I came to a large mesh that resembled a gigantic cobweb of intertwining dark strands. Membranes that were moving and pulsing with unnatural life were locked together and slithering all around me. I stopped and waited as a latent fear of spiders and snakes gripped me... but none came! Flashing green lights then began to dart sporadically through the sinister net and as they moved through the complex wire like the neurons of the brain, they seemed to guide my way...

I walked slowly deeper into the black web, cautious of every step as I was convinced that some unconceivable creature was lurking in the shadows, waiting for me to make a wrong move. I quickened my step but it was not the sound of some dormant spider I heard... it was a high-pitched hysterical laughter that was very faint at first, then as it came closer it became as irritating as an unwanted wasp at a picnic. Soft shuffling feet sounded behind me and I turned warily to see who was there but I could see nobody. The ghostly laughter continued to move around the web and amongst it I realized that I could hear music... drifting in and out and blending with the taunting laughter. I had heard this music before and after quickly searching my memory banks I realized that it was a track called Shadow from an early Eno album called On Land. Why the music of one of my favourite musicians was playing in the mind of another mystified me greatly but I had no time to worry about that, as the shuffling feet were getting closer...

Then I saw one of them... it was a small child dressed in the robes of a bygone age for some unknown reason. He ran in and out of the shadows as if he was teasing me, playing with me... and there were more of them. They knew that I was there and I was sure that they wanted me to follow them...

Through the darkness...
And the shadows and the music...

Then I could smell paint...
Fresh oil paint that had not dried...

I suddenly stepped into a small clearing where a group of children were standing in front of a large canvas. They were silent and still and this was ominous as the laughter had stopped but the music of Eno continued. Then the dull light slowly brightened until the painting was lit up before my unbelieving eyes.

The figures in the picture were life size and I had seen this painting before. It was the Martyrdom of Saint Matthew by Caravaggio, an artist I had studied at college. I knew that there was an inner darkness to a lot of Caravaggio's work and this was no exception. Saint Matthew was about to be killed by a scantily clad assailant, while a small angel reached frantically towards him from a lumbering cloud above... but it was not Saint Matthew lying helpless in front of the eager assassin, it was Reverend Robinson! ...His face was frozen and terrified.

I pushed frantically through the robotic children and as I did they quickly dissolved from my sight like ghosts fleeing the morning sun. I was now as close as I could get to the twisted work of art. The smell of oil and fear was overpowering... then the paint began to run. From the top of the towering canvas the colours began to slowly blend and then in rolling lumps they dripped down to the misty floor. The resulting blank canvas was not white as I expected... it was an unnatural black. I found myself standing in a puddle of red paint that was thick and sticky but it was not a mixture of oils I was standing in... it was blood!

I stepped out of the horrific pool and ran as fast as I could...
But my stride was dream-like...

My legs heavy...
My heart pounding...
And the childlike laughter had returned...
I began to panic...
But I kept going forward...
As best I could...
Further into the menacing mesh...
Until I could go no more...
I slumped to the ground exhausted.
And I think I slept.

When I awoke I knew that I had not been asleep long. Ambient music in the distance was beckoning to me. I knew that it was Eno's haunting Complex Heaven again and it acted like a beacon that I hastily followed... but I did not think that it was a complex Heaven I was heading to, it was more likely to be a complex Hell! ...Suddenly the music was louder and much clearer as I came upon a white door that surely signaled my journey's end. Immediately I heard his voice from within...

"Well, it seems you made it. Come Richard; please enter. Do not be afraid, at least not yet!"

I opened the door slowly and cautiously and I could feel my heart pounding like a distant drum that was trying to warn me. I had to keep my mind focused and be on my guard. Hunter had obviously possessed people before but for me it was too surreal, I was aware that my sanity was being threatened...

Inside, the room was not what I was expecting, in truth I really did not know what to expect and this was unsettling... the Ghost Train had reached it's destination and it was not scary! The room had the feel of a study or a dining room that was both homely and comfortable. Eamonn Hunter was sitting at the far end of a large glass table looking surprisingly debonair in a white dinner suit and black tie... I could have been looking at Bryan Ferry or Humphrey Bogart except his immaculately stylized hair was blonde. I was half expecting Hunter to say *Here's looking at you kid* and was very relieved when he did not...

"Sit down Richard, make yourself at home. The surroundings are most convivial, exactly what you would expect of a respectable young vicar are they not."

I sat down at the other end of the table directly facing him; I tried to appear calm but my pulse was racing. I could feel beads of sweat breaking out across my brow, I was scared but I did not want it to show. I wiped my forehead then looked nervously around me... to the right of me was a brown antique grandfather clock that was set against plush red wallpaper with a unique pattern. Repeated miniatures of the Crucified Christ subtly formed a Warhol-like design that was both intriguing and captivating. The old clock seemed to be too loud though and the tick tock of its ancient mechanisms became mesmeric and foreboding... then music filled the room and drowned out the sound of the hypnotic timepiece. It was not the music I had heard outside the room but it was the same artist...

"I hope you appreciate my choice of music... Neuroli by Brian Eno, quite apt don't you think?"

I ignored this irrelevant statement and then took the initiative...

"You defile a good vicar with your unwanted presence Hunter. What do you want to tell me, why have you brought me here?"

"All in good time Richard but first why don't you share some bread and wine with me."

On the table in front of Hunter were a large decanter of red wine and a freshly baked loaf; the aroma of both was very tempting to a stomach that had suddenly remembered that it had been grossly neglected. Next to the bread was a black Bible that was open as if Hunter had been reading it just before I had entered.

He sliced the bread with a sharp black knife that I seemed to recognize, an object from my imagination that was somehow symbolic. He poured me a large glass of wine then brought it to me with the bread. As he returned to his seat he asked a question of me...

"Why do you call me Hunter Richard?"

"That is the name you told me in your car..."

"Oh, of course but surely you do not think that I would reveal my true name to you? Eamonn Hunter is purely wordplay... quite witty don't you think?"

"Quite appropriate more like, Hunter seems just about right!"

"Touché Richard, touché... now where were we. Please let us enjoy the bread and wine together, I suspect that you have not eaten that much these past few days?"

"I will not dine with you Hunter... I am here for answers, not bread and wine...this is blasphemy!"

"How is that so? There is much you will never know about me Richard and anyway they were not my idea, they were already here with the Bible... quite a good read don't you think?"

"Stop playing games Hunter... I think we should start don't you?"

Hunter finished the bread he was vigorously chewing, and then drank all of his wine in one greedy gulp...

"Quite right Richard, quite right..." he spluttered, "I'm sure the Reverend has important work to do but he will just have to wait. Now where do we start ...how about the beginning?"

Suddenly he was dressed in the drab grey mackintosh coat he had worn at Ryhope Cemetery.

This stirred unpleasant memories in me; latent memories of a young boy aged nine or ten...

I was on the old bus again...
Heading for Sunderland town centre...
My faithful monkey following across the rooftops...
I think it was Sunday evening as the streets were deserted and quiet...
I was on my way to meet a friend...
He had recently moved from my street to a more affluent area.
We were going to the pictures together...
We were probably going to see James Bond or The Magnificent Seven.
The bus passed the Empire Theatre...
Then stopped...
I stepped off the bus and began to walk towards the Odeon...
And walking towards me... was a young man in a grey overcoat.
He stopped me suddenly and then asked...
    "Hello son, could you tell me where the Empire is..."
A stupid question but I did not realize it at the time...
I turned and pointed to the building behind me that was only a short distance away.
I walked on...
Then he came up behind me and beside me...
And began to talk...
Questions I did not like...
About school...
About being punished...
I quickened my step...
But he kept with me.
I turned into a small street, not far from the Cinema...
He was breathing heavily...

As he stepped into a shop doorway...
"Come son, let us talk more in here..."
"No... no... no way!"
I swore at him...
Then I ran, sprinting as fast as I could...
There was no way he could catch me,
I was a Sunderland Boys footballer...
I ran to the Odeon...
Where I met my friend...
I was shaken but I did not say anything...
"What's the matter Richie?" said my friend...
"You look like you have just seen a ghost!"

I felt a sickness in my stomach again...
"It was you! ...You were that pervert!"
"Yes Richard, our very first encounter... but I am not a pervert, I was just doing what I was told to do. Surely a teacher can understand that..."
"You evil bastard!"
"You know what, I am sure that you have called me that before somewhere..."
"So that is what you wanted me to know Hunter..."
"Oh there is more Richard, much more... please be patient with me. That night I followed you home and observed you and you know how easy that is for us. You became a... project, a target for the Dark Conscious. I had no choice in the matter..."
"Dark Conscious?"
"I see that all this is new to you but that is understandable, please forgive me."
He relaxed back into his chair and his despicable overcoat disappeared... there was a sickly aura about him; he had the look of a cat that was toying with its prey. He then pulled a thick cigar from the top pocket of his white dining jacket and lit it. Great clouds of smoke puffed into the air above him and partially

obscured his face...

"Lovely aroma isn't it Richard. Quite different from pipe smoke though, I think that smells much better don't you..."

I began to nervously sweat again as I knew what this was leading to...

"That was my grandfathers message to me... what do you know of that?" I shouted. A violent anger was building up inside me as I tried to control myself...

"Calm yourself Richard, I can see that you are shaking. It was your grandfather's message to you and quite clever and subtle it was too... brought to you by the courtesy of those annoying Blue Veins. Think Richard... who did you see that night, the night your mother died?"

I slumped back into my chair as I realized...

"You... it was you, you fiend!"

"Yes my friend. I am afraid I have been tormenting your family for years... it is something I am good at, am I not? What about your fathers father, another tragic road accident it would seem..."

I sat silent, my fists so tight under the table. Tears formed in my eyes as I thought of my mother and my grandfather, I began to imagine what he had done to them...

"And JJ, he managed to escape unfortunately... just like you did when you were young."

"The crash... you forced him to kill me... you were that old gypsy woman in London who cursed us. You've been persecuting us for years!"

"You are quite perceptive Richard but I am afraid this old woman you speak of was not me... probably just another servant of the Dark Conscious, we do tend to work together sometimes."

"So you wanted us both dead then, both at the same time?"

Hunter almost laughed out loud as he replied...

"Two birds with one stone? If only I was so clever..."

He could not control himself anymore and an evil laughter suddenly filled the room...

"No I only wanted to hurt your son JJ, the fact that it was you in the other car was just a pure accident if you will excuse the pun. It was a wonderful bonus though that earned me a lot of extra brownie points with my superiors..."

His prolonged laughter began to taunt me; then he continued...

"The purpose of killing JJ was to make you and your family suffer. However, I now get to watch JJ suffer instead, the fact that I revealed myself to him has made it so much sweeter. Win win situation Richard! Shall I run the reel? it makes for exciting viewing...

JJ was in his car...

A white mini cooper with the red cross of England...
Heading towards Castletown...
Speed limit 40 mph...
The hidden passenger was unknown to him...
He was listening to recordings of his own songs.

If you can breath then you can scream

Don't stop now when you've just got going
Your mind moves faster but your heart starts slowing

If you can sleep then you can dream
Memories mixed with hopeful intent
A nostalgical pulse from an imagined event
If you can breathe then you can scream

Take what's inspired and what you find
Declare I, dare I, one of a kind
You open up what's on my mind...

Near Red House, Hunter appeared...
JJ looked at him with cold surprise...
Wide eyes staring in disbelief...
Was his mind playing tricks?
He had not been drinking...
No tricks though... it was Hunter!
Evil smile...
Evil laughter...

I know your father JJ...
And I know your grandmother too.
You like metal JJ?
Lets turn it up!
Lets speed things up!

Hunter's foot hit the pedal...
50, 60, 70...
100... 120...

Now we're Rockin' JJ...
Look, we've even got a light show...

Pot holes appeared in the road...
Blue lights, green lights...
Shooting up to the sky...
Twisting and tangling...
Discord... tension...
The Mini swerved past a black Station Wagon...
JJ released his belt...
And opened the door...
A split second...

And he was out...
Rolling across the road to safety...
Hunter rolling with him...

The white Mini Cooper...
Hits the black Fiat Punto...

Darkness...
Then light...
Not white light... it was blue.
Then it turned darker... almost green...

"So you see Richard... just damned bad luck, that is all. For once the Blue Veins failed you!"

I sat still... as silent as the dead. It is not every day that you get to watch your own death! I felt a gagging in my throat; my mouth was dry... I could not speak. I looked to the grandfather clock that was ticking like a church bell... it was nearly midnight.

"I suppose you want to kill me now Richard? You might be doing me a favour if you succeed... or perhaps it will be you who will die?"

The clock struck midnight with the sound of a giant alarm bell... and I remembered the young girl in Devils Wood...

"No... I am not here to kill you Hunter, I am here to tell you that she forgives you."

A surprised look crossed his face...

"Who forgives me? ...Your mother?"

"Yes, she probably does too... but it is not my mother I refer to though, it is a young girl called Rose! You killed her in Devils Wood didn't you! Cut the poor souls throat like a blood orange... then buried her like a dead stray dog amongst the winter leaves."

Hunter stood up, his eyes were red and burning...

his features changed instantly and he became Demonic... like he was the one now possessed!

Slowly, from his body came the Black Wire... emerging from his head then writhing like living snakes all around him. He reminded me of some warped Medusa, intent on turning me to stone. If I was going to freeze with fear then this was the moment. The Dark Conscious was taking control of him...

"What do you know of Rose!" he demanded with a voice so deep that seemed to be rising from the depths of Hell. This was pure anger like I had never seen or known before. He swept his arm across the table sending the bread and wine crashing to the floor...

"Tell me... Tell me feeble one!"

I had pushed a red button in him, touched some long forgotten hidden nerve... perhaps one of his many Black Wires...

He grabbed the Dark Dagger and came at me, pushing the glass table onto its side... a million sharp fragments flew against the wall in a slow motion that was reminiscent of an action movie and immediately I heard a low moan, scared and pitiful echo around the room. I knew it was Reverend Robinson and this possession; this conflict was something he could not stand much longer... then a blue light began to emanate from me. Hazy strands that were translucent sprang from me, from the top of my head like electricity... the Blue Veins began to fill me with strength and a renewed vitality...

"You will tell me before you die, the Dark Conscious demands it!"

...He hit me full on my bruised face and I fell from my chair. He then sprang at me like a demented Vampire and grabbed me by the neck, I gasped for air as I gripped his wrists...

"What do you know of Rose!" he demanded again.

I spluttered and formed my words as best I could...

"She forgives you Hunter... but I do not!"

I kicked him as hard as I could between the legs, my steel toe Doctor Martins finding the desired target. His pain was palpable as he dropped the knife... I picked it up quickly as he began to fall on top of me. I slashed his throat with the black, sharp blade...

"This is for Rose, evil one... and my family!"

I did not know what to expect... dark red blood gushed from the cut onto my shaking hands... Hunter gasped in pain, his red eyes revealing fear and absolute terror. I did not know how old he was but it was time that he was no more...

Clean Hands and Dirty Hands...

He slumped over me, finally lifeless... he seemed taller and was much heavier than I expected. There was not much blood though but enough to make me sick... my empty stomach emptied what it could onto his cold, motionless frame. I pushed him aside and stood up shaking like a soldier who had just made his first kill...

I stood there for some time, trying to make sense of what had happened... I had just killed somebody or something, an evil that had been part of my life for years, unknown and unforgiving. Suddenly there was a crackling noise above me that sounded like a distant thunder... light flashed throughout the room in the form of forked lightning. A blue light then formed above Eamonn Hunters body... surely not I desperately thought! Why would the Clear Conscious want him?

"No!" I shouted abruptly, "No he is not worthy!"

Then a green light appeared and filled the room. The Black Wire was back and it crawled with menace towards Hunter. Across the floor it slithered, like a pack of large hungry snakes approaching their prey. The Blue Veins had attached themselves to Hunter and were trying to lift him towards the ceiling... but the Black Wire now had their revolting tentacles beneath his body and was pulling him back down.

This sight sickened me as I expected his phantom body to burst open at any moment. The Blue Veins flashed like lightning again but the vile green light only became thicker and stronger... like a solid force expanding within the room. It pressed against me hard and tried to crush me like I was an intruder. I could hear the Reverend's voice outside of me; calling, crying... I had to escape. I staggered out of his mind and back into the church...

Reverend Robinson had collapsed in front of the Altar; he was alive but unconscious. He was murmuring like he was having a bad dream and his body was twitching uncontrollably. He needed medical help immediately. I went to the Vestry and phoned for an ambulance, then left the church when I heard the siren. It was better that I should not be seen, a ghost in a churchyard? ...Now who would believe that!

Chapter Twelve

WASHINGTON LIBRARY

There was only one person I could trust to believe this story, one person that had to... and that was my eldest son Robert. I had silently checked on Reverend Robinson and found out that it would be a few weeks before he would show any signs of recovery. The Doctor had put it down to the possible stress of a new job and workload, a diagnosis that is perhaps a little too prevalent these days. Obviously then, I could not risk his help with JJ now so there had to be another way... and this is it.

This story is for you Robert. You must show it to JJ. He was not to blame for my death, as you now know. Everything he said was true; there was something in the car with him that fateful day... something evil that I have now vanquished. I have put things right as you must do now; it is the only way we can help JJ.

I know what you may be thinking, that this is some sort of twisted wind up... but you must understand that I could not simply reveal myself to you as that would have caused untold chaos as I am sure you are now well aware. If you still do not believe in ghosts, then let this photograph be my evidence...

You might have seen this picture in the Echo or on Look North; two boys on their way to Oxclose School took it. They had found me after I had crashed into that oak tree and took the photograph on their mobile phones as I was waking up.

Look Robert. Look at the hands of The Devils Wood Ghost...
My SAFC ring...
My silver card ring...
My Tigers Eye heirloom ring...
And on my chest... my silver Saint Christopher and silver Cross.
I am that ghost Robert and everything in this manuscript is true!

This story then, is for you and JJ alone (unless of course, you think you can make any money from it... Hollywood here we come!)

So finally son, we will meet again one day and hopefully not too soon. Both of you have a full life ahead of you, make sure you enjoy it and live it to the full. Remember… be not afraid.

    Hey, Let it Rock!
    God bless,
    Your loving Dad.

Now all I want to do before I return is Google Jeanette Alderson…

Acknowledgments

Many thanks to: -

Steve Nanson - Front Cover Art Direction/traffic direction and encouragement.

Matt Nanson - nanson.eu - Front Cover Photography and Art Direction... the cheques in the post.

1. Dracula - Bram Stoker - Archibald, Constable and Company.1897.

2. Nosferatu The Vampyre - F.W.Murnau - Film Arts Guild. 1922.

3. Strange Case Of Dr Jeykll And Mr Hyde - Robert Louis Stephenson - Longmans, Green & Co. 1886.

4. The Fantastic Four - Stan Lee/Jack Kirby - Marvel Comics.

5. Nick Cave - Clean Hands Dirty Hands - The Proposition. 2005.

6. Stanley Myers - Cavatina. The Deerhunter.

7. Brian Eno - Always Returning. Apollo. 1983

8. Family - Burning Bridges - Roger Chapman/John Whitney. Fearless. 1971.

9. Bryan Ferry - Walk A Mile In My Shoes - South - Another Time, Another Place. 1974.

10. Bob Dylan - Things Have Changed – 2000

11. The Doors - Riders On The Storm - Jim Morrison. L.A. Woman. 1971.

12. J.J. Cale - Travelling' Light - Troubadour. 1976.

13. Star Trek - Gene Roddenbury. 1966.

14. Roxy Music - The Bogus Man - Bryan Ferry - For Your Pleasure. 1973.

15. Bryan Ferry - Song to the Siren - Buckley/Becket - Olympia. 2010.

16. Anna Calvi - Desire - Anna Calvi. 2011.

17. The Wild One - Laslo Benedek - Columbia Pictures. 1953.

18. The Black Rebel Motorcycle Club - Need Some Air - Baby 81. 2007.

19. Batman - Bob Kane/Bill Finger - DC Comics. 1939.

20. Family - In My Own Time - Roger Chapman/John Whitney. 1971.

21. The Invisible Man - H.G. Wells - C. Arthur Pearson - 1987.

22. Family - The Breeze - Roger Chapman/John Whitney - Music In A Dolls House. 1968.

23. Brian Eno - Shadow - On Land

24. Brian Eno - Complex Heaven - Small Craft On A

Milk Sea. 2010.

25.Family - Hey, Let It Rock - Roger Chapman/John Whitney - A Song For Me. 1970.

26.James J. Snowball - Inspired. 2012.

27.Ryhope In Old Picture Postcards - J.N.Pace - European Library.

Author's Note

Complex Heaven is a work of fiction. However, true-life experiences are included throughout the book but I will let you the reader, be the judge of what is real or what is imagined.

My references to music are essential to my story and I would like to again acknowledge the artists mentioned. Their song and inspiration is central to the creative process in both my artwork and in my writing and I consider myself lucky to have lived in the Golden Age of Rock.

Certain place names have been changed throughout the novel due to the involvement of imagined characters but I must acknowledge the existence and beauty of St. Paul's in Ryhope, Sunderland… a church that my mother Elizabeth always held dear to her heart.

The eternal battle still rages…

Richard Valanga.

26th September 2012.